KINGPIN WIFEYS
SEASON 2
VOLUME 5

BY

K. ELLIOTT

April 2015

CONTENTS

KINGPIN WIFEYS II,
Part 3: Going Hard

Chapter 1

"WHAT'S IN YOUR HAND?" STARR ASKED.

Q held onto the locket. "A locket." He exposed the locket in the palm of his hand.

Starr reached for it, wanting to take a closer look, but Q held onto it for a while before finally releasing it.

Starr smiled and said, "A baby."

"Yeah, that's Rico's daughter, Ivy, as a newborn."

"She's beautiful."

"She's a woman now."

"Why do you have it?"

"I'm her godfather."

"Did something happen to Rico?" She passed back the locket.

"No. Why do you ask?"

"I don't know. You were in a kind of reflective state."

There were so many thoughts racing through Q's head. He was anxious, but he had to stay cool in front of Starr. There were lots of questions that needed to be answered. What would he do with Rico's head? Did Rico suffer before dying? How in the fuck would he tell Rico's family and what was he going to do about it? The cartel had literally beheaded his friend.

"How did you get it?"

"He gave it to me a while ago."

The FedEx box sat on a wooden chair in the corner of the room. Starr inched toward the box and scooped it up, but before she could sit down,

Q snatched the box away.

"What's in the box?" She eyed him suspiciously.

"Nothing. Valuables."

"Breakable?"

"No."

"You didn't have to snatch it. I would've given it to you."

"Look. I'm sorry."

"What is it?"

"Art my friend brought me back from South Africa."

"Do you mind if I take a look? I might get some ideas for by business."

"Not right, now. Let's get dressed and go to breakfast."

"It's only going to take a minute."

He smiled and said, "Look, I don't want you to see what's in the box because it's a surprise that I have for you. I'm working on something and I'll show it to you later."

She smiled and said, "It better not be expensive. I don't want you to try to buy my affection, Quentin."

"I thought I had your affection."

"You do, but you know what I mean."

Q held the door and she sprang from the desk. They showered, got dressed and headed to Gladys Knight's for chicken and waffles.

Chapter 2

TODD LEFT MIKE'S WIFE AND SON LOCKED IN A WALK-IN CLOSET. *HE* drove to Dunwoody, and helped Dank load the three bodies into the car, and then they drove them to South Carolina where they disposed of them in Lake Hartwell right at the Georgia/ South Carolina line.

The next day, at TeTe's orders, Todd and Dank began looking for Shakur. They purchased a membership to L.A. Fitness, the club where Shakur was also a member. They could have waited in the parking lot, but they didn't want security to get suspicious. They worked out twice the first day waiting on Shakur to arrive, but he never showed. Nor did he show up the next day.

On the third day, they watched as he came into the club dressed in Under Armor tights. They watched him workout from across the room as he flexed his biceps and took selfies in the full-length mirror. One thing for sure, he was in love with himself.

They laughed at his silly ass as he did set after set of grueling exercises. Barbell curls, bench presses, squat lunges and swimming. Then he showered and made a beeline to the Yoga Studio around the corner.

"This nigga is a workout fanatic." Dank said.

They stayed on Shakur and waited as he did his Downward Dogs and Sun Salutations. An hour later, Shakur emerged drenched from the hot yoga class. He jumped into his silver Maserati and exited the parking lot.

Todd pulled alongside him and Dank fired eighteen bullets into the side of Shakur's car. Three bullets ripped into his chest and one bullet blasted the side of his head. Shakur crashed into the side of a 7/11 store.

When the store manager realized what had happened, he struggled to open the door of Shakur's car. Once he had it open, the manager hopped into the car and slammed it into park, then he dragged Shakur out the car. Shakur had lost a lot of blood but his eyes were open and he was still breathing. The manager ordered him to breathe and breathe. Shakur tried but the side of his head was severally damage and his brains were spilling out.

A store worker said, "It's over, man. His hair is on fire."

Shakur's dreads were sizzling and seconds later he took his last breath in the store manager's arms. His silver Under Armor shirt now a maroon color.

Todd and Dank exited on Interstate 85 and were heading toward the house in Dunwoody.

Todd said, "You think we got him?"

"I got him. He's dead by now."

"You're confident."

"Nobody survives a bullet to the head."

"All that goddamned exercise didn't do his strong ass no good in the end. All that lifting and walking around the gym in tight-ass spandex swimming and shit. Flexing with his shirt off and taking selfies."

"Doing yoga and shit. Gay-ass yoga."

They were laughing their asses off at Shakur, knowing that when they reported back to TeTe, she was certainly going to be happy with them. They would be paid well.

Chapter 3

BLACK HAD PURCHASED HIMSELF A BURNER PHONE FROM WAL-MART.
He was feeling pretty good that TeTe had taken revenge against some of his enemies, but he had to admit to himself that he was a little afraid of her. She was very calculating and manipulative. He knew that she liked him but wondered what would happen if he crossed her. He'd seen a side of her that he was frightened of, but nevertheless, he was glad that she had murdered his adversaries.

He had business to take care of and there was no way that he would be able to take care of his business and watch his back at the same time. He had a new connect. A good connect was the one thing that he'd never had. Black drove to Hopkins and Adair in South East Atlanta to see a guy named Melvin Beatty, nicknamed Popcorn.

Hopkins and Adair were two intersecting streets in Atlanta and in one of the worst hoods in the United States. It even came with crime statistics to back this assertion up. In other words, you didn't want to be there if you didn't have any business there. You would absolutely get your cranium cracked, but Black knew it well. He used to go with his dad to do business back in the nineties.

Today, he had to catch up with his friend, Popcorn. Black used to do a lot of business with him before he and Shamari delved into the world of heroin. Popcorn was a mid-level dealer that wanted everybody to think he was big time. He owned seven cars and all of them white. They surrounded a tiny little shack that he rented in the middle of the hood, situated between two boarded up houses. Black parked in front of Popcorn's house and spotted Popcorn's nephew, J.J., bouncing a basketball doing freakish, wicked crossovers.

J.J. was six foot six and seventeen years old. He sported a goatee and looked at least twenty-five. Damn near every college in the country was recruiting him to play for them. He was a sure shot for the NBA if he could stay out of trouble and stop smoking weed. Two things that he had not been able to do thus far.

J.J's father was in prison for shooting a man in the back and paralyzing him from the waist down. Popcorn's sister, Michelle, gave him the task of making sure J.J. stayed out of trouble and attended school until he left for college. Uncle Popcorn was an ex-con as well as a crack and Molly dealer with three baby mamas—-a really great role model for the kid.

J.J. wore black and gray Jordan's, True Religions with a Hermes belt that one of the rich white girls at the school had bought him. He clearly wasn't using it since his pants were sagging so low his whole ass was on display.

He approached the car, the sun directly in his eyes. J.J. squinted as he tried to get a clear look at Black.

"Go get Corn for me. Tell him it's Black," Black said.

J.J. and Black had never formally met but J.J. did recognize Black. He'd surely seen him before. Dropping the ball, J.J. sprinted up the stairs that led to the dilapidated shack.

Moments later, Popcorn marched outside wearing house slippers and white, oversized thermal underwear. Popcorn's skin was the color of butter. The guy had bad skin from drinking too much and had very unkempt cornrows. He was slim with a ballooned stomach.

Black lowered his window and said, "Corn, it's Black."

"Oh, I didn't know who the fuck you was."

"I told J.J. to tell you it was Black."

Popcorn lit a Black and Mild cigar as J.J. started bouncing the ball again. Popcorn started looking annoyed.

"Hey, man! Can you wait until me and Black finishing talking?"

J.J. said, "Unc, let me hit the cigar."

"Hell the fuck no! Come on, man. How the fuck are you going to be Lebron if you wanna smoke every goddamned day? You think Lebron smoking? You think Seth Curry smoking cigars?"

"You mean Steph?"

"Same thing. They brothers, ain't they? Neither one of them is smoking. They somewhere shooting jumpers and shit. You ain't even on their level and all you want to do is smoke cigars and weed and fuck bitches."

J.J. bounced the ball again and this further irritated Popcorn. He passed him the cigar and said, "Now get the hell away from here and let grown men talk."

J.J. let go the ball and scooted away inhaling the cigar.

Black said, "You're too hard on him."

"Not hard enough. This boy got a million-dollar talent, and he's going to fuck it up and end up in the streets like me and you."

"Don't say that."

"It's true, Black. He's had full scholarships to two prep schools and got kicked out of both of them."

"Damn."

"So where you been?"

"Trying to go legit. Well, I was trying. I invested in a few restaurants."

"That's what's up. So, what brings you here?"

"Opportunity."

"What kind?"

"Good coco prices."

"I'm going to be honest, man. Word in the streets is that you ain't right."

Black looked confused. "What da fuck do you mean that I ain't right?"

"I heard that you set this dude up and he got life. And he's in the Atlanta Pen right now."

Black couldn't believe what he was hearing. He wanted to hop out of the car and slap the fuck out of Popcorn for even questioning his street cred.

"Look, bruh, I'm just telling you what I heard. The streets is saying that you got some dude named Shamari life."

"I just sent Shamari some money the other day. Shamari is my partner, man. I've never done anything to him. Somebody else set him up. He'll tell you that."

"For real?"

"You know I don't get down like that."

"I'm just telling you what I heard."

"I'm telling you that what you heard was wrong."

"My cousin Junior is in the Atlanta Pen. I'm going to tell him to find Shamari and ask him about it."

"Tell the motherfucker to find him, and after he finds him, you call me. Maybe, we can do some business."

Popcorn was analyzing what Black was saying and he certainly sounded convincing. Finally, he said, "Look, Black, I believe you."

"If you believe me, why the fuck did you bring it up to me?"

"I was just telling you what I heard."

"So do you want to see what I got or not?"

"What's the price?"

"Thirty."

"A little high."

"For pure shit?! Get the fuck out of here! Right now you can't find that shit in Atlanta for under thirty-five."

Popcorn knew what Black was saying was true, but that didn't mean that he wasn't going to try to get a lower price. The lower the price, the bigger the profit.

"So when can I see what you got?"

"What do you think you will buy?"

"Two or three if it's pure. I don't have the bread, but I got a friend that's been calling me from Memphis. I can get his bread."

"I have to go home and get it. I will be back on this side…" Black glanced at his watch, "I'm going to say around five o'clock."

"Perfect."

Black sped off in a hurry, still upset that Popcorn had questioned his street cred, but now was not the time to get emotional. He knew that he didn't owe nobody an explanation for what he had done and fuck anyone that would question his street cred.

Chapter 4

FRESH EXITED THE ELEVATOR THAT LED TO Q'S PENTHOUSE. Q unlatched the door and let him in.

"What's wrong?" Fresh said as he marched right past Q into the living room. He sat down on a leather armchair.

"He's dead."

"Who's dead?"

"Rico, fool, Who else?"

"What do you mean he's dead? And how do you know?"

"My office is the third door on the left. Go open that FedEx box on the chair."

Fresh looked confused, but he did as he was told and a minute later, he sprinted back and said to Q, "I didn't want to see that."

"I didn't want to see it either, but I had to see it." Q paused.

Fresh paced and cracked his knuckles. He was nervous as hell and he needed to calm the fuck down. He needed to smoke, but he was sure Q didn't have anything. He only smoked cigars and he needed something much stronger than that.

"I can't believe the motherfucker reneged," Fresh said.

Q sat there with his hand between his legs and he said, "You don't even know the half."

"It can't be worse than what I already saw. Nothing can."

"You're right. Personally, this is one of the biggest losses I've ever taken. I was devastated when Trey got murdered, but Rico was really like family. We grew up together. Me, Rico, your Uncle Kevin. We were like brothers."

"We gotta make this right."

"What do you mean?"

"We gotta get even, bruh."

"I was thinking the same thing," Q said. "You know I don't give a fuck about Diego, but there is no way that we're going to get to him. We'll get killed."

"So does Rico's family know that he's dead?"

"No. And I'm wondering what the fuck are we going to do with his head? We gotta get rid of it. We can't let them know how he died. No way."

"They don't need to know that," Fresh said, then he remembered that Q said that he had more bad news. "You had something else to tell me?"

"Oh yeah, I almost forgot."

"Forgot what?"

"The coke is worthless."

"What you mean worthless?"

"It's mostly sheetrock."

"Who said so?"

"Eric called from North Carolina and Marcellas called from New Orleans."

Fresh stood and said, "Did you call Diego?"

"The phone is going to voicemail, but do you really think he's going to do something about it now?"

Fresh removed his iPhone and called, trying desperately to reach Diego, but he got Diego's voicemail as well. Now, he was pissed the fuck off.

"Q, we can't let this motherfucker get away with this. We've lost millions of dollars. We gotta deal with his ass."

"How?"

"You know he'll be at that slut's restaurant sooner or later."

"His sister, Anna. I hadn't thought about that."

"We gotta get somebody to spray up the goddamned restaurant! Customers and all!"

"We can't do that."

"I don't give a fuck about them damn wetbacks." He sat down on the arm of the sofa beside Q. "We can't let this ride, Q."

"You're right."

"Call Black and let him know that the shit is not right before he tries to make a move with it."

Fresh dialed Black's number but got sent straight to voicemail.

Chapter 5

BLACK PHONED L FROM HIS PHONE, BUT L DIDN'T ANSWER. HE figured that L didn't recognize the number. He'd hoped that L wasn't out sticking people up. He drove to Sasha's house to pick up the coke that he'd stashed. As he was getting on the elevator he received a call from L.

"Hello?"

"Somebody call L?"

"It's Black."

"I didn't recognize the number."

"Where you at?"

"I had to go see my daughter. I'm about to head back to the house."

"Slacking on the job again, I see."

"Ain't nobody slacking. I'm not supposed to have a life?"

"Of course, you can have a life. I just wish you would have called me before you left."

"I did. Your phone was off."

Black knew what L was saying was true. That particular phone had been powered off all day. "Okay, I'll meet you at the house later tonight."

"Okay. I was going to ask you for a favor."

"What?"

"My car broke down and I had it towed to the shop. I was going to ask if you could rent me a car. I'll give you the money for the rental. I ain't got no credit card."

There was no way in hell Black was going to rent L a car. Though L was forty-five years old, he wasn't responsible.

Black said, "Look, L, I don't have a credit card, either."

"Can you pick me up and drop me off at the house?"

"Where are you?"

"I'm over by the A.U. center. As a matter of fact, just pick me up at the West End Mall."

That was perfect for Black because Popcorn twenty minutes away. He could pick L up on his way to sell the dope to Popcorn.

An hour later, Black arrived at the mall. L was standing out front with his backpack on. He hopped into the Camaro.

Black said, "What's wrong with your car?"

"I don't know. I ain't no mechanic. I think it might be the radiator. It was running hot and shit."

L adjusted the seat.

Black was eyeing the backpack and noticed that it was stuffed so he asked, "L, what's in the backpack?"

"Clothes."

"Lemme see."

"What the fuck? You don't believe me. I get it. You think I've been out here robbing."

L glanced at Black and they made eye contact for a moment then L turned away. He unzipped the backpack and there were two T-shirts, a pair of Jordan's and a .45.

"Why do you have a gun?"

L chuckled and said, "What the hell?" You think I ain't supposed to have a gun with me. I got enemies, remember? Just like you got enemies." L paused and then said, "Do you mind if I zip my backpack up...Dad."

"Very funny."

"You think you're my daddy, but I'm fifteen years older than you."

"Look, L, I just don't want anything to happen to—"

"Us. Don't say you don't want anything to happen to me because, Black, you could give a flying fuck about what happens to me. You just don't want big, stupid L to go out and get arrested."

Black powered the radio up. Rae Sremmurd's "Throw Sum Mo" was playing and they rode in silence for about ten minutes before L noticed that they weren't going in the direction of the house.

"Where we going, bruh?"

"I gotta make a play."

"Make a play? Fuck you mean, make a play?"

Black lowered the volume "What do you think I mean by make a play?"

"We riding with dope."

"Yup."

"Ok, so it's okay for you to have dope on you and you question me about a gun?"

"Look, L, when I take you back to the house, I'm going to pay you for the job and you go the fuck on about your business."

"Fine with me, bruh, fine with me. I don't need you telling me what the fuck I can and cannot do."

Black blasted the radio. Big Sean's "Blessings" was now on. Neither man said anything for the next ten minutes and finally Black parked on the side of the road in front of the steps that led to Popcorn's house. Popcorn's nephew, J.J., sat on the step with his teenaged girlfriend between his legs. His basketball a few feet away.

J.J. and his girl stood. She leaned into him and kissed him while he gripped a handful of her ass. Her tight skinny jeans made her ass look fantastic. Black thought back to when he was in high school. Those were the days. Though he was sure the girls that went to school with him weren't built like J.J.'s girlfriend. She kissed him again before strolling up the sidewalk. Black and L both watched the seventeen-year-old's ass sway before the sound of the bouncing basketball snapped them out of their trance.

Black lowered the window and said, "Is Corn in the house?"

"Yeah, I'll go get him." J.J. disappeared into the house and returned a minute later. "He said to come inside."

Black turned the ignition off and grabbed the overnight bag with the two bricks of coke from under the seat. His gun was on his waist. His leg was still hurt from the accident so he grabbed his crutches and pulled himself out of the car.

He took the stairs that led to Popcorn's house and inside, he saw Popcorn and an unfamiliar man playing Madden on the PS4. Black never understood how guys in their thirties would spend all day playing a childish-ass game.

Black eyed the stranger before saying, "Corn, I didn't know you had company."

"It's okay. This is my man, Memphis."

Memphis made eye contact with Black. Memphis was a dark man. Almost as dark as Black. Bloodshot eyes and a Cro-Magnon head, He had gold front teeth and was wearing a Tupac T-shirt, jeans and Jordan's. He and Black shook hands.

Black said, "Corn, can I talk to you for a second?"

Popcorn paused the game and turned to Memphis and said, "Hey, I'll be right back."

Black followed Popcorn into the kitchen and secured the door. Black said, "Who the fuck is this dude? You know I don't do business with new niggas."

"I've known Memphis for years. He's cool, bruh. Trust me. Plus, I don't have that kind of money. But he does. He's alright. Man, he just looks shady, but I swear to you, I've counted the money."

Black eyeballed Popcorn. He certainly didn't want to have to carry the product back with him. He wanted Fresh and Q to give him more product.

He wanted to live like Trey had lived. He had to prove that he could handle what they had given him so that he could build more trust. They would watch him closely.

Popcorn said, "Look, Black, there ain't gonna be no funny shit. This nigga drove all the way from Memphis."

"Memphis? How did he get here so fast? I just told you that I had product a few hours ago."

"He's been here for two days looking for coke, bruh. No shit. I've been looking for him and then you came this morning and said that you had product. That was perfect because he was about to head back. We just counted sixty grand right there in my motherfucking living room floor. My nephew saw it. I'll call J.J. right now to prove it."

Popcorn removed his cellphone from his pocket and Black said, "That's okay."

"Can I bring Memphis back?"

"Yeah."

Seconds later Memphis was in the kitchen and Black was staring at his head thinking, this nigga got the biggest goddamned head he'd ever seen in his life.

Memphis unzipped a backpack and Black kept his eyes on him the whole time, hoping that this dude didn't have a gun. When he saw the stacks of money, he relaxed. He removed the coke from his overnight bag and put in on the table.

Memphis said, "We're going to cut that open, right?"

"Black said, "One of them is already opened."

"Can I see it?" Memphis asked.

Black passed him the one that he'd tore into early. Popcorn handed Memphis a pair of scissors and he tore into the packet and dabbed the product with his thumb and tasted it. The face that he made afterward let Black know that he was utterly disgusted, but Black didn't think nothing of it because coke's taste was disgusting and numbs your tongue.

Memphis said, "This ain't coke, man."

"What are you talking about, man?" Popcorn said.

Memphis said, "Yeah, your man is trying to get over on me."

Corn said, "Let me taste it." Popcorn knew exactly what coke was supposed to taste like and when he tasted it, he said, "This ain't it, bruh."

"Hell, no! Let me taste it." Black reached for the coke and he scooped a little bit up with his finger and put it in his mouth. "You're right, and I'm sorry, man. I'm sorry."

Black wondered what the fuck was going on. Was Fresh trying to get over on him? But for what reason? He hadn't given them any money.

Memphis removed a chrome .45 and aimed it at Popcorn's head. "Yo, what the fuck y'all trying to prove, Corn?"

Popcorn threw his hands up and said, "Look, man, I ain't know nothing about this."

Memphis pointed the gun at Black and ordered him to get in a corner beside the fridge. Black wanted to reach for his gun, but he knew that if he did, he would surely get shot. So many thoughts ran through his mind. What the fuck had happened to the coke? He had never tasted the coke or had it tested. He had just assumed that it was good because, after all, Q was Trey's connect. His eyes were on the barrel of that chrome .45. His life was in a total stranger's hand—a stranger that not only didn't know him, but thought that he was trying to fuck him out of his money. He was surely going to die and this was not the way that he'd envisioned going out.

Chapter 6

JADA WAS LYING IN BED BUTT NAKED, HALF-ASLEEP AFTER SENDING Fresh some sexy pictures. He loved the pictures, but he protested that she didn't send pics of her face. She'd replied that she didn't send pics like that to nobody that wasn't her man. Her phone rang and she was disappointed when she saw it was Big Papa and not Fresh. She rejected his call and sent his fat ass straight to voice mail, but then he called Jada three times back to back. She wanted to keep avoiding him, but after he called the fourth time, she picked up.

"Hello?"

"Can I see you?"

"I'm in bed about to go to sleep."

"It's about Shakur."

"What about him?"

"I don't want to talk about it on the phone. Can we meet up or no?"

"Yes...Sure...Where?"

"Let's meet at the IHOP downtown. How long will it take you to get dressed?"

"I can be there in a half hour."

"Okay."

So many things were running through Jada's head. What was going on with Shakur and why wouldn't Big Papa tell her? She knew how he never talked on phones and how paranoid he was about the Feds. He believed everybody was trying to set him up, but she had to give it to him, though he was slow when it came to dealing with women, he was a genius at going undetected. With the exception of his cars, he rarely spent money unless it was on his children or on women who were using him for his money. She slid into some Victoria Secret pink sweatpants and a pair of Uggs then she brushed her teeth and whipped her hair into a ponytail.

She didn't feel cute at all, but hell, she wasn't going nowhere but IHOP. She headed out the door and fifteen minutes later, she was walking into IHOP. She spotted Big Papa's fat ass stuffed in a booth in the back of the restaurant, eating some grits and bacon along with an order of pancakes. As soon as she sat in the booth, the waitress, a perky little strawberry blond named Samantha, asked Jada if was she ready to order. She only wanted a water with lemon and Big Papa asked for a diet coke to go along with his feast. As if the fact that the diet coke had zero calories mattered given he was well over fourteen hundred with one meal.

After Samantha returned with the diet coke and the ice water, Jada said, "Why was it so important to see me?"

"Shakur is dead."

"Please, tell me you're kidding?"

"I wish I was kidding." He looked like he wanted to start crying and Jada believed him.

"How did it happen?"

"That's what I want to ask you."

"Wait a minute! He was murdered?"

"Yes." Big Papa ate a spoonful of grits then took a swig of diet coke and said, "Yeah, he was murdered yesterday."

"How did it happen?"

"Someone pulled alongside him and sprayed his car and he crashed into a 7/11."

"You're lying."

Big Papa let go of his spoon and said, "Jada, I'm not kidding. Why do you keep saying that?"

"You think I had something to do with it?" Jada asked.

"I think you know who did."

"You think I know who planned it?"

"Look." He paused then scanned the restaurant. "I don't know."

"This is real fucked up," Jada said. She placed her hands on the table then her phone fell through a hole in her pocket. Big Papa tried to pick it up but he couldn't reach it with his stubby arms and he almost tilted the table over. The grits slid to Jada's side of the table. She fished her phone over with her feet and slid Big Papa's grits back to his side of the table.

Big Papa painted his pancakes with butter then drowned them with maple syrup without looking at Jada.

"I'm the one that tried to diffuse the situation before it came down to this. Do you remember when I came to your condo and I had you call Shakur?"

Big Papa didn't respond. He didn't make eye contact.

"Don't you remember that?"

Finally he locked eyes for a while. "I do, that's why I feel like you know who did this."

"I have no idea."

"What about Black?"

"What about him?"

"Where is he?"

"I don't fuck with Black."

Big Papa knifed the pancakes into itty-bitty pieces. "Look, there a lot of gangsters upset about Shakur's murder and they're asking about you."

"Gangsters? Asking about me?"

"Because when you chose to try to squash the beef apparently he told some of them that Black had sent you over."

"But he didn't."

Big Papa took another drink of the diet coke and let out a nasty-loud, disgusting-ass burp. "But that's what they think."

"So, I'm involved?"

"Yep."

"But you know I didn't have shit to do with it."

"I don't know shit."

"Look, you fat motherfucker. You need to go and tell them that I ain't have shit to do with it. You know I didn't want anyone dead."

"So, is that what you think of me?"

"Huh?"

"You think I'm a fat disgusting motherfucker. Go ahead and say it, Jada. You think I'm fat and you would never have anything to do with me."

"Wait a minute! What are we talking about here? Shakur's death or whether or not I like you?"

"Look, I just never expected you to call me a fat motherfucker."

Jada could see that she'd really hurt his feeling and she was really regretful for calling him out. He'd been really good to her and he didn't deserve that.

"I'm sorry."

"It's okay."

"No it's not. I'm sorry and I'm sorry if you felt like I've been using you."

Big Papa said, "Look it's okay, Jada. I allowed it to happen. But like I was saying, there about twenty niggas from Detroit wanting to know who you are and where to find you."

"Did you tell them who I was?"

"Of course not."

"What did you tell them?"

"I told them that you're a stripper from LA."

"Did they believe you?"

"I don't know."

Jada thought the last thing she needed was a bunch of hooligans after her, thinking that she had something to do with a murder.

She said, "Look, I swear to you. I didn't know anything about this."

Big Papa gulped down the diet coke. He rattled the ice that remained in the cup and it was getting on Jada's goddamned nerves.

"Could you please stop?"

Big Papa let out a loud disgusting burp and said, "My bad."

Jada stared him in the eyes searching for clues as to what he was thinking. He began rattling the ice again before sitting the glass on the table. Finally, he looked at her and said, "I believe you."

"You're the only person that I care believes me or not."

"Why is that?"

"You're a good person."

"I try to be."

Jada stood and leaned into Big Papa and bear hugged him. "I gotta go now."

He watched her ass as she walked toward the door but he wasn't lusting. He was over her. Big Papa paid the tab and made his way slowly to the parking lot. He looked around and then got into his car. He watched as two masked men fired sixteen shots into Jada's car. Glass shattered. Tires blew out.

Big Papa screeched out of the parking lot as a tear rolled down his cheek. This would be the last time that he saw Jada. But he didn't have a choice after five Detroit goons showed up at his house saying that he either took them to Jada or they would kill him and his kids. He thought they didn't know where his kids resided, but when one of the men blurted out the address, he knew that they were serious.

He didn't want to set her up. He didn't want her to get murdered, but it was either her or him and she'd used him. She took his money, had played him with no intention of fucking him. All she had ever did was take from him so the decision was easy. He got Jada to come over to the IHOP so she would park in the back of the dark parking lot and the assailants could roll up and spray her vehicle.

He was half way up Peachtree when he pulled to the side of the road and cried. He would miss the hell out of that girl. Though she'd used him, he loved her and he couldn't help it.

Chapter 7

IT WAS NINE A.M. AND AFTER DROPPING T.J. OFF AT SCHOOL, STARR drove straight to Q's house. He was surprised because he wasn't expecting her. She walked into the living room and sat on the sofa. He plopped down right beside her. He leaned toward her and gave her a passionless peck on the jaw.

"What's wrong?" Starr asked.

"Nothing."

"Look, I was just thinking about yesterday. You were acting weird as hell. I couldn't put my finger on it."

"I'm sorry."

There was an awkward silence and she finally said, "Do you think we're doing the right thing?"

She could tell by the look on his face that he was very perplexed. She said, "Do you think we're doing the right thing by trying to be together? I mean you have things to do. Business to take care of. Lots on your mind. You're a business man, baby. You don't have time for me. I don't feel wanted and I don't know if I can deal with that."

"So what are you saying?"

"I don't feel like I'm in a real relationship."

"You want something to drink?"

She laughed. "I just tell you I don't feel like I'm in a real relationship, and you offer me a goddamned drink!"

"You just said the other day you didn't think nobody could make you love them after Trey, until I came along."

"I love you, Quentin."

"And I love you."

"I just don't feel loved."

He sighed then ran his fingers through his hair. Searching for words to put her at ease. Words to let her know that she was the most important person in his whole existence besides his children. But he couldn't find the right words. He disappeared into the kitchen to get a drink and when he reemerged, she was crying.

"What's wrong?"

"Nothing." She stood and made a beeline toward the door but he cut her off. He sat his drink on the table and wrapped his arms around her waist to comfort her. He'd been around enough women in his day to realize something was terribly wrong whether she said it or not.

She tried to push him away. "Let me go, Quentin."

"Not before you tell me what's wrong."

"So, you haven't been listening to me?"

"I have."

"You haven't been hearing me."

"I heard you, and I can understand why you feel this way."

"But you don't want to do anything about it."

"About what?'

She was frustrated as hell. Talking to him was like talking to T.J. except T.J. comprehended way better than he did.

"There is something I've been keeping from you," Q said.

Starr's heart fluttered. What the fuck did he have to tell her? Another kid? He'd told her about his children. His baby mamas. She hoped this motherfucker wasn't married. If he was married she would fight his ass for playing with her heart. As much as she hated it, she had to admit that she'd grown to love this man and she would be devastated if he had lied to her. She'd been lied to so much by Trey and she didn't have time for another grown-ass man playing silly-ass games.

There was a long silence and Starr finally said, "Q, what is it, goddamn it? What is it that you have to tell me?"

He attempted to touch her arm to calm her down and she pushed his hand out the way and said, "Don't touch me. Tell me what you need to tell me."

"My friend was murdered."

She stared at him for a while. She was glad that it wasn't another woman. She was glad he wasn't married but she didn't expect him to tell her that.

"What?"

"Murdered. And I didn't want to tell you."

"Why? Why wouldn't you tell me?"

"Have a seat."

She sat down and he said, "You remember the last time you stayed over?"

"Yeah."

"Remember when you came into the office and there was a box sitting on the desk?"

"The box that you said contained a surprise for me?"

"Yeah. I lied about that."

"Why?"

"The box had my friend's head in it."

"His head? Huh? What?" This whole thing wasn't making no sense to her.

"They decapitated him, bruh."

"I'm not a man. Don't call me bruh."

"Forgive me."

Starr sighed and said, "No forgive me for acting like a bitch."

"It's okay.

"Who does shit like that?"

"These people." Q made his way over to the window and peered out into the Atlanta night. Starr followed him and wrapped her arms around him. Her heartbeat was in sync with his, and at that moment, he felt safe. He felt loved and he wasn't worried about the cartel or anybody. He didn't care if he had money or not. All that mattered was that she was there with him and he had been honest with her. He'd told her what he was going through and she was still there for him. He turned and kissed her.

She said, "So what are you going to do, baby?"

"I don't know what to do."

"I know you're upset that your friend is gone, but at least you're out the game now."

"I don't know about that. I lost ten million dollars."

"What? How did you lose it?"

"Look, I don't want to get all in to it. But long story short, I put up some of my money so that they would let Rico go and they didn't do what they were supposed to do."

"I'm so sorry."

"It's not your fault."

"You have to walk away from this before you lose your life."

"I can't."

"Why not?"

"I have to get the man who did this to Rico. I have to. I can't let this shit ride. I know that this is not what you signed up for and I apologize to you for this. And as much as I would like to think of myself as something else, no matter how many businesses I have, no matter how much money I have, I'm still the same old street nigga from Fifth Ward."

"You choose to be."

Q pushed Starr away and said, "If they shot him and killed him that would be one thing but to decapitate my friend, they were trying to send a message and I'm going to send a message of my own."

He and Starr locked eyes and held for a very long time and she knew that he was serious about what he'd just said. She just didn't know if she wanted to be a part of his life.

Chapter 8

"WHAT THE FUCK HAPPENED TO MY CAR?" JADA SAID AS SHE EXAMINED the shattered windows, the flat tires and the bullet holes that riddled the side door. "Somebody help me! Help me!"

Two young girls approached Jada. A white one and a black one. They looked to be at least twenty years old. The chubby black girl had braids and braces with an oval face.

She said, "Me and my friend saw the whole thing."

"What did you see?"

"You were in your car for a couple of minutes and it looked like you were looking for something."

"Yeah, I left my cell phone inside in the booth so I jumped out the car and ran back inside."

"As soon as you went back inside, a Dodge Ram pulled up."

The white girl said, "That was not a Dodge Ram. My dad has a Dodge Ram and that was some kind of Chevy."

"Whatever," the black girl said. "The point is a pickup truck pulled up beside your car and sprayed the whole goddamned car. There were two men."

"How did they look like?"

"They were wearing masks," the white girl said.

"Not ski masks. Black bandannas covered their faces," the black girl said.

"So, you didn't get a good look at them?" Jada asked the black girl.

"No, not really."

Jada dialed Big Papa's phone but he didn't pick up. She called him again.

No answer. The police were called to the scene of the shooting, and by the time they arrived, a crowd had formed around the car. Everybody asking what happened.

The manager, a tall, slinky white guy with unkempt brown hair described to the police what he'd heard. And he kept on and on about how nothing like that had ever happened in the IHOP parking lot. He told them that he'd worked in IHOPs in three different cities and a whole bunch of irrelevant details and finally the cop had had enough of his slinky ass and wanted to speak to the owner of the car.

Jada approached Officer Mark Shannon, who was young and handsome as well as buffed and tanned. Though it was nighttime, a pair of Oakley sunglasses rested on the top of his head. He looked like the kind of white boy that would be surfing if he lived on a beach.

"So what is your name, ma'am?"

"Jada Simone."

"You want to tell us what happened?"

"Isn't it obvious?"

Officer Shannon realized that it was a stupid question and he chuckled just a little—not because anything was funny but because he was embarrassed.

The chubby black girl came over and said, "I saw the whole thing."

This surprised Shannon because most of the black youth that he had come in contact with never wanted to be a witness to a crime.

"Is she with you?" Shannon asked Jada.

Officer Shannon thought that they were together because they were both black and it was obvious. He wasn't racist though. He'd actually banged a few black girls and had even been engaged to one before she cheated on him with a basketball player. Now, he was happily married to a white girl.

"No, we're not together."

Officer Shannon asked the black girl for her name.

"Brianna...Brianna Thomas."

"Tell me what happened, Brianna?"

"I saw her get into her car and she was looking around for something, like she'd lost a wallet or something. Me and my friend was about to ask her if she wanted help finding whatever it was that she was looking for."

Jada interjected, "I was looking for my phone. My pocket is ripped and my phone slipped out. Thank God."

"Then what happened?" Shannon asked the girl. "Why didn't you go and help?"

"Before we could, she ran back inside the restaurant."

"Back inside?" He turned to Jada.

"Yeah, I'd just met a friend there earlier and I went back inside to see if I could find my phone."

Officer Shannon turned back to Brianna. "Continue."

"Moments after she was inside, not even thirty seconds later, two men wearing bandanas drove by in a pickup truck and opened fire on the car."

"What kind of truck?"

"I thought it was a Dodge Ram, but my friend says it was a Chevy."

"Your friend? What friend?"

Brianna pointed to the scared white girl gazing across the parking lot, not wanting to be involved. She was afraid that if she snitched, gangsters would come looking for her because that's what they did on the movies. That's what happened on The Wire. She wanted no part of that lifestyle.

Officer Shannon waved Brianna's friend over and she came over hesitantly. Her name was Lorie Donnelly. She was nineteen and tall with blond hair and freckles. She had huge muscled thighs. Lorie was a volleyball player from Wisconsin and she attended the University of Georgia on scholarship.

Officer Shannon forced Lori to give her account of the story and Lori said the same thing that Brianna had said except she was sure the truck was a Chevy. Officer Shannon thanked the girls, sent them on their way, and said that he would be in touch if he needed them.

Then he asked Jada, "Can you think of somebody that wants you dead?"

"No," Jada lied as she thought back to the conversation with Big Papa. He'd said that the Detroit boys were looking for her.

"Well, it's obvious that somebody does."

Jada looked at her Benz riddled with bullet holes. She wanted to cry but couldn't bring herself to do it right now. It was not the time to be weak.

Officer Shannon said, "Is there anything at all that you want to tell me? Anything at all?"

"I wasn't here. I was inside so I don't have anything to offer you other than what I already told you."

"Your friend?"

"What friend."

"The one that you met here. Where is he?"

"I don't know. He left."

"Do you think—"

Jada cut him off. "I don't think he had anything to do with it."

"How are you so sure?"

That was a good goddamned question. How was she sure? He was gone. He wasn't answering the phone and it was him that invited her here. Then it dawned on her. Big Papa's fat ass had tried to have her murdered.

"What is his name?"

"Ty."

"Last name?"

"I don't know." Jada had known his last name but she couldn't think of it right now. So it was simpler to say that she didn't know.

"Can you call him?"

"I tried. He's not answering."

"Can I have his number?"

Jada gave the police Big Papa's number. Ordinarily she would have nothing for the police but his fat ass had tried to have her murdered and right now she didn't give a fuck about him.

"Do you have a ride home?"

"I can call someone."

Shannon passed Jada a card and said, "Get in touch with me if you remember anything that you think is relevant."

"I will."

Chapter 9

THERE WAS A CHURCH'S CHICKEN CUP IN THE CUP HOLDER AND L had to piss. He wasn't familiar with the neighborhood. He didn't want to get out of the car to take a piss. This was the hood and there was a definite possibility that the police were patrolling the neighborhood.

When he couldn't wait any longer, L sprang from the car and eased to the side of the house to take a piss. While there he heard Black say, "Nah, bruh, it ain't even like that. Come on. Bruh, it ain't worth it. I'll make it up to you."

Then he heard another voice say, "Motherfucker, you tried to get over on me. You tried to beat me out of sixty grand and it's niggas like you that fuck the game up."

L peeked inside the window and saw Black backed into a corner at gunpoint. The man with the gun had his back toward L and his face wasn't visible. But L could see that rather large head.

L removed his gun from his waist and aimed the gun at the man's head. L knew he had one shot and if he missed, Black would be dead. He focused and fired. Seconds later, the hollow point bullet burst into the back of the man's head.

Memphis plummeted to the floor. L ran to the back porch and kicked the door in. He found Black and another man inside the kitchen. L fired two shots which exploded into the other man's chest.

Black said, "L, how did you know?"

"I was taking a piss and I heard you arguing."

"Let's get the fuck out of here."

L eyed the backpack with the money in it and said, "I'm taking this money with me." He grabbed the backpack.

"What happened?" L said. Cocaine was spread all across the old kitchen table.

"Let's just get out of here. I'll tell you in the car."

Black searched around for his crutches, but couldn't find them. He could barely walk. L scooped him up in with one swift motion and tossed him over his shoulder. L was walking out of the house when J.J. ran up the stairs with the ball in his hand. L let go of Black as L and J.J. made eye contact. L sat Black on the porch and aimed the gun at J.J.

When Black realized what was going on he said, "No L. Don't do it. He's just a kid."

It took every ounce of strength in Black's body for him to stand, but when he stood, he grabbed L's hand and said, "Get the fuck away from here, J.J."

J.J. sprinted away, but L broke free from Black and fired two shots into J.J.'s back. J.J.'s body hit the side of the steps and the ball bounced away. Black hated that L had murdered Popcorn, and especially J.J., but he knew it had to be done. When they were back inside the car, Black sped off as he tossed his cell phone out of the window to get rid of all correspondence with Popcorn.

When they were back at the house, L said, "What was that all about?"

"Bad coke, man."

"Huh?"

"I didn't know. I thought it was good."

"But they thought it was bad?"

"It was bad. When I tasted it, it didn't taste right."

"What happened?"

"I don't know."

"Who did you get it from?"

"New connect."

"You think they got over on you, bruh?"

"I dunno."

Black powered on his old cell phone and called Fresh. He answered on the first ring.

"Yo. Why haven't you had your phone on? I been trying to call you all day, trying to tell you that that cake was stale." Black knew right away that that was code for the coke was bad.

"I just found out. And I found out the hard way. Almost got killed."

"What?"

"I'll tell you when I see you."

"Damn!"

"It's okay, bruh."

"You sure?"

"I'm positive." But Black knew it was not okay. Three people were killed and he was sure that the police would be after his and L's ass sooner or later. He would have to lay low for a while.

TeTe had been shampooing Butterfly's hair but left the bathroom to open the door. When she opened the door for Todd, she noticed Butterfly had trailed her, shampoo spilling on the floor. TeTe turned and kneeled so she was eye level with her daughter. "I'm going to need you to mop this damn soap up and rinse your hair and dry it before I whip your ass and take your cell phone away. Understand me? Now me and Uncle Todd has something to discuss, okay?"

"Why can't Auntie Lucille clean up?"

"Cuz I told yo ass to do it. You're the one that made the mess, so you do it. Understand me?"

"Yes," Butterfly said.

"Yes what?"

"Yes, ma'am." Butterfly said. Then she disappeared to retrieve the mop. TeTe led Todd into the den and latched the door.

"What's wrong?"

"Is it that obvious?"

"You showed up unannounced. You never show up unannounced."

"The police came to Dank's house and picked him up. Said he was a person of interest."

"Why did they pick him up and not you?"

"I have no idea."

"Is he still in custody?"

"Yes, but I don't think he's been charged yet."

"Okay, I'm going to get my attorney to take a look into this."

"Yeah. We gotta get him out."

"Well, if he hasn't been charged with anything, there is no way to get him out yet."

"You're right."

"Do you think someone got your tag number when you went to visit Mr. Shakur?"

"Impossible."

"Why is it impossible?"

"We had the tag covered."

TeTe said, "Don't worry. I'll get to the bottom of this."

The next day, Todd came over and TeTe told him that Dank was going to get charged for suspicion of kidnapping and murder. Apparently the dumb motherfucker had dropped a McDonald's bag with a receipt in the front yard of Mike's house and the cops were able to check the time of the receipt and verify that it was him on the camera at the store. Mike's wife identified him as one of the men that had forced her to take him inside their home.

"Damn."

"Why the fuck did y'all dumb asses have to go to McDonald's?"

"His idea. He was hungry."

"I should leave his fat ass in there."

"But who knew that they would find a receipt?"

"They are the fucking police. It's their job to find clues and it's our job not to give them any."

"So what's next?"

"We are waiting for them to set a bond and then we'll have to get him out."

"A goddamned receipt from McDonald's." Todd thought back to the day and he remembered when Dank tossed the bag on the lawn of the house.

"We gotta get his ass out before they realize that he had something to do with the other two bodies," TeTe said.

"Three." Todd said.

"Three?"

"Shakur?"

"Damn, I forgot about him." She laughed. "I guess he doesn't count in my mind cuz I didn't even get to meet Mr. Shakur but I'm sure he's entertaining his friends now." She laughed aloud again. "Dank's bond will probably be around a million cash so he needs someone to sign for him. I'll put up the money, but he's still going to be on house arrest. And then they may revoke the bond if the charges are upgraded to murder which I'm sure they will be eventually."

Chapter 10

AFTER L MURDERED POPCORN, HIS NEPHEW, AND MEMPHIS, BLACK knew that the car was no longer safe to drive. Someone may have seen them leaving the scene. He stashed the car at his father's junkyard and borrowed his dad's F150.

His father looked at Black and said, "If you get me in some bullshit, I'm snitching on yo black ass. I'm too old to be going back to prison."

Black knew that Bankhead Bo meant exactly what he said. "Don't worry, Dad. It'll be okay." Then Black drove off to meet Fresh.

Fresh said, "Still on the crutches I see."

"Yeah but I can walk a little bit better now. I really don't need them."

They were at the Atlanta Bread Company on Piedmont Ave. The cashier gave them a number and they took a seat in the back of the restaurant. Fresh had ordered a pepperoni pizza and Black had a roast beef sandwich. Both had Sprites.

"What was that all about? I thought you said you were Trey's connect. I heard Trey had the best shit."

"We're going through some shit right now. I promise it will get better."

"I almost got killed."

"What do you mean? You almost got killed?"

"Just what I said. This dude from Memphis held me at gunpoint. He'd brought sixty thousand dollars over to make a play. But when he tasted it and found out that it wasn't right, he drew his gun on me. I'm telling you, bruh, he was going to kill me."

The server dropped the food and removed the number from the table. "What happened?"

My man L was still out in the car and heard the commotion. He peeked in the window and saw me in trouble.

"How did you know this dude?"

"I didn't. He's a friend of a friend."

"So you were at your friend's house?" Fresh peeled a slice of pizza off the tin pan and stuffed it down his throat.

"Yeah."

"What happened to your friend? How did he feel about your boy L killing somebody in his house?"

"He was fucked about it. Of course, he didn't want it to go down, but he understands how it happens sometimes," Black lied.

Black intentionally left out that L had murdered two other people. He didn't want them to feel uncomfortable. He still wanted them to supply him. He had plans for taking over Atlanta and he needed them to do it.

Fresh studied Black's face to determine if he was lying. He sipped his Sprite and then said, "I'll talk to Q and we'll make it up."

"When?"

"A week or two."

"Why did this happen?"

"It was a bad batch. It happens from time to time."

"I'll never make that mistake again."

"What mistake?"

"Selling something that I haven't had tested."

"Look, you'll never have to test anything. We are always a hundred percent pure."

"You dropped the ball this time."

"We did, but we're going to make it right. Watch."

"Have you seen, Jada?" Black asked.

"No. I'd planned to call her tonight."

Black had been planning to call Jada as well because he was almost sure that Jada had heard about the murders of Mike, Kenny Boo and Tater. He wanted to tell his side of the story and he didn't want her to tell Fresh about it.

• • •

Three hours later, Black rang Jada's doorbell repeatedly. Her car was gone, but a black Mercedes was parked out front. He knew the car didn't belong to Fresh. He was in a rental but it wasn't a Mercedes. Maybe she had a new man. Maybe somebody else was banging her besides Fresh. It was certainly possible. She was a fine motherfucker and she's never been a one-man woman. But then he thought if this was the case, her car would still be home but it was gone. He was about to turn and walk away when he heard the door creak open.

"What the hell you doing here, Black?"

"I need to talk."

"Of course."

"Can I come in?"

Jada thought about cursing him the fuck out and sending him on his way, but Shakur had been murdered according to Big Papa and she needed to know what happened. She led him into the kitchen. She placed a white Tupperware dish filled with mac and cheese that her mom had made for her into the microwave. Two minutes later, the bell rung and she removed the mac and cheese. Steam was rising from it. It was piping hot. She offered Black some but he declined and said he'd been to the Atlanta Bread Company earlier.

The mac and cheese smelled delicious, and Black said, "Hey, as a matter of fact, I do want some. That shit smells great."

Jada wanted to tell the motherfucker that he couldn't have any. The truth was she was happy that he'd declined the first time, but instead she got a bowl out of the cabinet and forked over half of it into the bowl for his greedy ass.

"I thought you were going to curse me out."

She gave him a fake smile. "I'm glad you came."

Black was eating that mac and cheese like he hadn't eaten in days. Jada had thought he'd said he had just eaten at the Atlanta Bread Company, but Louise's mac and cheese had that effect on people.

Black stared up from his plate briefly and said, "Damn, this shit good. Who cooked this?"

"Me."

"You ain't cook this."

"I could have." She smiled.

"You could have, but you didn't."

"Look, my mama cooked it, but I know you ain't come over here to talk about no mac and cheese."

"I didn't."

"What do you want?"

"I need to tell you something."

"What?"

"Look, that girl, TeTe. She's not like us."

"What do you mean us?"

"She's not normal."

"Why do you say that?"

"She killed Mike, Kenny Boo and Tater."

"Who the fuck are they?"

"Mike is Chris's brother. Kenny Boo and Tater were Mike's friends."

"TeTe killed them? No way."

"Jada, I'm telling you what I saw. I witnessed it."

"But why are you afraid? I don't get it. Didn't you want them dead?"

"I did, but who would think a woman would do that? Women don't do shit like that. Women don't murder in cold blood unless there is a husband involved. Crimes of passion and shit like that."

"Never underestimate a woman."

Black finished eating the plate of macaroni and asked for some water. She passed him a bottle and said, "So TeTe did everything, and you didn't have anything to do with any of this."

"It's the truth." He took a swig of water and then said, "I'm not saying I'm not happy that she did it."

"I find it hard to believe that a woman is going to go find men and kill them."

"Look, she has her own goons."

"Goons?"

"Dudes that protect her and carry out hits for her. This ain't a regular woman, Jada. I'm telling you."

"I wanted to ask you something."

"Anything."

"Who murdered Shakur?"

"Nobody."

"Wrong! Shakur was murdered a few days ago. TeTe ain't tell you?" Jada said sarcastically.

"This is the first I heard about it, but maybe she did. I haven't talk to her in a couple of days, but if I had to bet, I would say that she did it."

"There are a lot of dudes from Detroit right now, riding around Atlanta thinking that I know who murdered Shakur."

"Who said that?"

"Did you not notice that my car is not in the driveway?"

"I did. Is it in the shop?"

"My car was shot up the other night. Somebody tried to kill me."

"What?"

"Yeah. They thought I was in the car and tried to murder me."

"Damn!"

"Damn, my ass, Black! I need to know what the fuck happened."

"I swear to God, Jada. This was all TeTe."

"Shakur?"

"She was looking for Shakur."

"This don't sound right?"

"I've never met anyone like her."

Jada was still eating her mac and cheese and she said, "Look, I like Fresh." Black said, "That's none of my business."

"I'm glad you feel that way because I really like him—in a way I didn't like Shamari. Don't get me wrong, I love Shamari and I'll always be there for him. I don't give a damn if they keep him locked up for a thousand years, but I don't love him like I like Fresh. If that makes any sense to you."

"I understand, but why are you telling me this?"

"I don't want Fresh to know that my car was shot up. Can you promise me that you won't tell him? You know that's a bad look for a girl."

"He's going to notice that you don't have your car."

"I'll tell him it's in the shop."

Black said, "I promise not to mention it, only if you don't mention what's going on with me."

"You got it."

Jada's phone rang. Shamari. She didn't want to answer but she hadn't spoken to him in a while and she could let him speak to Black.

"Hello?"

She didn't wait on the recording to tell her that she had a call from a correctional facility. She pressed five right away and was connected to Shamari.

"Hey, bae."

"What's going on out there?"

"Same old same."

Black said, "Let me speak to him."

"Who is that?"

"Black?"

"Again?"

"Don't start with me."

"Hand him the phone."

Jada passed Black the phone.

"Black boy, what's up?" Shamari said.

"Trying to make it."

"What do you mean, trying to make it? You're free, at least."

"Yeah, I guess so."

"What's up with Jada?"

"What do you mean?"

Jada stared him right in eye.

Black said, "Call me later, man. At my new number. I'll leave it with Jada. Let's catch up." He passed the phone back to Jada.

Jada said, "Call me back in fifteen minutes, baby. I need to finish talking to Black."

"What the fuck you gotta talk to him about?"

"Look, I'll come up there on Saturday to tell you all about it."

"Tell Black I said I'm going to call him later. Tell him it's going to take about a week to get the new number on the phone list. They will have to approve it first."

"Okay, baby." Jada terminated the call. "I'm trying to be patient with this motherfucker. I'm trying to be there for him and he keeps acting like I owe him something. Every time he calls me, it's like fifty motherfuckin' questions." Jada paused then said, "Black, you know me. I'm going to be there for him. I love him, but I'm not going to stop my motherfuckin' life. No way."

"Look, I'll talk to him when he calls me."

"Somebody better talk to this motherfucker before I end up blocking him from calling me."

Black laughed his ass off. Then he said, "Jada, you're a good person and I'm going to get the people that did this to you."

"Black, leave it alone. Let it go."

Black stared at her for a while then said, "Are you going to eat the rest of that mac and cheese?"

"Boy, if you don't get your black ass out of here, some damage is going to occur."

He shrugged. "Had to ask. Tell you Mom that's some good stuff and that she's the real MVP."

They both were laughing like hell.

Chapter 11

AS SOON AS GORDO'S FLIGHT ARRIVED AT HARTSFIELD INTERNATIONAL Airport, he phoned Q but there was no answer. He called Fresh and Fresh told him to get a room at the W on 14th street.

Gordo, dressed in a black cowboy hat and snakeskin boots, checked into his room then went to meet Fresh at Whiskey Park, the bar inside the hotel. Gordo had a vodka tonic and Fresh had a Hennessy.

"Can you get Q to come over? I've called him four times and he won't pick up," Gordo said.

Fresh dialed the number and Q answered on the first ring. "Can you meet me at the bar inside my hotel? I need to talk to you about something."

"Give me thirty minutes."

Gordo gulped his drink and said, "Look. I'm very sorry for what happened to your friend. I had nothing to do with it."

I believe you." Fresh paused, stirred his liquor before taking a swig and said, "You made us a promise that you didn't keep."

An awkward silence. Gordo avoided eye contact with Fresh.

"You didn't try to stop it?"

"Diego lied to me. Our uncle is very upset with Diego. He knows Q is a good customer and a trustworthy man. He has made Diego leave the compound."

"And you believed Diego?"

"Didn't you?"

"Well, I believed him because we'd worked together for so many years together."

"I'm sad for your friend," Gordo said.

"It was fucked up," Fresh said. He stirred his drink.

"Yes it is. It's very bad."

"And on top of that, he sent bad coke. And he knew he sent bad coke."

"What? I didn't know. I'll be sure to tell my uncle and we will try to fix the mistake."

"It wasn't a mistake."

"My English is not best."

"We're out a shitload of money."

Gordo sipped his drink. He didn't know what to say to make Fresh feel better. He'd hated things had turned out like this.

Q approached the table before recognizing Gordo. As soon as he saw Gordo, he turned to walk away. Gordo ran out and jumped in front of him.

"I want to talk," Gordo said.

"Talk." Q said.

"Can you sit with us?" Gordo pointed to the table.

Q sat beside Fresh, across from Gordo, and then he said to Fresh, "Why didn't you tell me he was here?"

"Because you wouldn't have come."

'That's for damn sure."

Gordo said, "You want a drink?"

"I don't want no goddamned drink. I can buy my own if I wanted one."

"Look, I'm very, very sorry about what happened to your friend."

"He has a name."

"I'm sorry for what happened to Rico."

Q eyed Gordo and deep down inside, he knew that Gordo was really sorry for what happened. But it had happened and Gordo had said that he would make sure that nothing happened to Rico. He didn't do what he'd promised and for that, Q was pissed.

Q said, "So what do you want?"

"I want us to help each other."

"Look, you can't bring my friend back. So there's nothing for me to talk about."

"Look, I know you're hurting right now, and I can imagine how much pain you must be in right now."

"Can you imagine?"

"I've had worse. My father was murdered when I was five years old and I cried for weeks. My father was my best friend. My hero. I hated God for a long time for what I thought he did to my father."

'What changed?"

"My father was a member of the cartel, and I realized that God didn't have anything to do with it. We make choices. My father made a choice for this lifestyle. I made a choice. You made a choice."

"Now I'm choosing to leave it alone."

"You can try to run but you can't run from yourself. This is what you were meant to be."

"Huh?"

"Listen, we need each other."

"What the fuck do I need you for?"

"If you help me, I'll get my cousin. I'll bring you his head for what he did to you."

"And what about my money?"

"How much did you lose?"

"About ten million."

"I can't pay you ten million dollars, but I'll give you a thousand kilos on consignment for what I get them for."

"How much do you want for them?"

"Seven thousand. This is the price I get them for, but I will keep the price very low until you make your money back."

"When are you going to send them?"

"That's the problem. I don't have a way to get them here. I thought you moved your own drugs."

"Rico did all that."

"So how did you get them here last time?"

"I used a moving company. They never knew what I was shipping. Shipped it inside the furniture."

"Can't you do the same thing this time?"

"Too risky."

"I have a friend in New York. He uses private planes. Why don't you lease a private plane to move the product?"

"In my name? Get the fuck out of here."

"Find somebody to do it."

"I'll think about."

"Think about it and give me a call."

"I will."

Chapter 12

BLACK WAS LYING ACROSS HIS BED AT HIS HOUSE FACE-TIMING WITH his daughter Tierany. TeTe was calling him back to back. He called her up as soon as he ended the call to Tierany. She answered right away.

"Hey, bae! Where you been?"

"I've been here. Working."

"Like you have a real job." She laughed.

"And like you have a real job."

"I'm a business woman."

"Is that so?"

"I handle my business and you know it."

Black sat up bed and said, "That's for damn sure."

"I was hoping I didn't scare you."

"You didn't," Black said. The truth was that he wasn't scared, but he did realize that she was bat-shit crazy. He was crazy too and he knew that together they were lethal, but part of him still wanted her.

"Come work for me."

"Work for you?"

"Yeah, I want you to move in and fuck me good and get paid for doing so."

He laughed and said, "You think you can buy me?"

"I was just saying."

"It's not an option."

"So you'd rather risk your life dealing?"

Black was stunned that this crazy bitch was thinking that he was risking his life. Like there was no possibility that she would ever get caught for doing what she was doing? Like she would never go to prison.

"Why don't you come over? I have a surprise for you."

"A surprise?"

"Yes. Do you like surprises?"

"Who don't like surprises?"

Black stared at the clock and realized there was nothing that he had to do. There was no work and he was bored. He said, "Give me an hour."

"Bring your things over. I want you to stay the night with me."

"Where is your daughter?"

"She's with my sister."

"I didn't know you had a sister."

"Yes, I have a twin. She's a travel nurse, so I don't see her much."

"Interesting."

"Why do you say that?"

"I just didn't know you had a twin, that's all. Do y'all look alike?"

"Yes, we're kinda the same but we used to look more alike when we were younger."

"I'll be there soon."

Four hours later, Black arrived at TeTe's house. TeTe opened the door wearing an elegant, long, light-blue sheer nightgown. The Roots singing "You Got Me" played through her surround In-wall speakers. Grown-ass woman, Black thought. Crazy but grown.

This was the first time that Black had actually seen a woman in a sexy nightgown. Most of the women that he'd dated were young and they wore thongs and boy short lace panties. But here was TeTe, who was clearly disturbed, wearing a sexy, elegant nightgown. Looking very sophisticated and innocent. Like she was incapable of harming anyone or anything. She bear hugged him and he could smell a mixture of Love in White and Aventis by Creed and it was turning him the fuck on.

"Did you miss me?"

"I did," he said.

Once he was inside, she closed the door. Her ass bounced as she led him to the den. Her fragrance lingering in the air. His dick sprang to life. He wanted to fuck her right then and there but he hadn't showered and she smelled like a floral arrangement.

When they were seated in the den, she said, "I almost forgot."

"Forgot what?"

"The surprise, silly goose."

"I thought you were my surprise, with your delicious-looking ass."

She smiled, clearly turned on by him.

"I'm only part of the surprise."

He laughed as she stood up and made her way upstairs to the bedroom. Moments later, she returned with a Neiman Marcus bag and passed it to him.

He removed a motorcycle jacket. "Damn! This thing is nice."

"Ballenciaga."

"Damn! It must have cost a few grand."

"What's a couple of thousand dollars spent on somebody I like?"

"You're trying to buy me." He smiled and then laughed. When he made eye contact with her, he realized that she wasn't laughing. She was frowning. Clearly pissed the fuck off. What the fuck?

Her hands were resting on her hips. "This is the second time you've said that. I don't have to buy anybody. I'm not one of those desperate, thirsty young girls that you're used to."

Black laughed and said, "Calm down, ma. It was just a joke."

"I am calm. Believe me; you'll know when I'm not calm."

Black was silent for a moment. Something clearly wasn't right with this woman. He made his way over to a mirror that was beside the fireplace and modeled the jacket. He had to admit the jacket was fly as hell. She had great taste.

He turned to her and said, "I love this jacket. I wouldn't have never thought to buy something like this but it works." He smiled. Then he moved toward her and leaned into her and gave her a peck on the cheek. "I love it, baby."

"Glad you like it."

He tried to kiss her lips and she shoved him backwards.

"What's wrong?" Black asked.

She slipped away from him and said, "I can't get over the fact that you said I was trying to buy you. I don't need to buy a man." She turned and made eye contact with him and said, "Do I look desperate?"

"Look, baby, I was just playing."

"Don't play with me like that." She curled up on the sofa like a kitten. "I was trying to give your ass an opportunity, if nothing else."

"What do you mean?"

"Help me run my business, so you won't be on the streets."

"I got my pride. I don't want no woman taking care of me."

"There are a lot of prideful niggas in the pen."

"We just killed three people."

"I killed three people."

"Right."

"Look, I'm not crazy. When somebody tries to hurt me, I hurt them."

"Well, they tried to kill me."

"Like Slick always told me, bullets don't have names on them."

"Who the fuck is Slick?"

"The man that taught me everything I know."

"Look, I'm sorry that I got you involved."

"You don't have to be sorry. That's part of the game. Sometimes you gotta do what you gotta do."

Black made his way over to the sofa and he slid his hand underneath her gown until he found her thong. He slipped his finger inside her kitty and finger fucked her until she exploded. A thick white sheet of cum covered his finger and she licked it off. Then they kissed and he kicked off his shoes and undressed. It would be a fun-filled night after all.

Chapter 13

INSIDE FRESH'S HOTEL SUITE, BLACK, FRESH AND Q SMOKED expensive cigars and sipped Cognac as they sat in the living room area watching the Hawks play the Thunder.

Q said, "Look, Black, I'm so sorry about what happened. This will never happen again."

"What are you talking about?"

"The bad dope, man."

Fresh said, "He almost got killed, right, Black?"

"Damn."

"Yeah. Dude thought I was trying to beat him for sixty grand."

"What?"

"Yeah."

"He pulled his gun out on me and everything."

"What happened?"

"My man shot him."

"Did he die?"

"Yeah, he died but nobody saw it." Black lied. There was no way he was going to admit to the other deaths. He knew that if he revealed to them that L had murdered three people that would be the end of their relationship before they even got started good and he needed them. He'd seen from afar how good Trey had lived and he'd secretly envied Trey. Though he did well for himself, he'd never reached the success in the drug game that Trey found, and he knew Q was the key to that success.

"Damn." Q said reflective, trying to decide if he believed that nobody saw the murder. The story sounded vague like Black was leaving out some details. "I'm sorry this happened to you."

"So, when are we going to get back on task?"

Q sipped his liquor and said, "Look, we have a problem, and I was wanting to know if you could help us."

Black blew a cloud of smoke and said, "What's the problem?"

"We need help with transportation."

"Look, I don't know anybody that can help us with that. I'm sorry." For a brief moment, Black thought about the trips that Shamari and Jada had made to Cali.

"Well, we don't need you to go."

"I don't understand."

"We need somebody to charter a plane in their name. Can you help with that? Somebody with a Platinum Amex."

Black thought for a moment. He could ask his sister, she had A1 credit but he knew the answer to that. She would curse him the fuck out. She still wasn't over the fact that the authorities had questioned her about Chris's murder. Then he thought about his baby mamas. All them bitches' credit scores together still wouldn't be above five hundred, so that was out the question.

Fresh said, "Do you know anyone?"

"I'm still thinking."

Black said, "What about Starr?"

"You know damn well Starr is not going to do this," Q said.

"So what will they have to do exactly?"

"Just use their Amex to charter the plane and I'll pay them for the use."

"So how much is it going to cost."

"Around forty grand."

"And what's in it for the person?"

There was an awkward silence in the room. Fresh and Q looked at each other. They obviously hadn't thought about what they would give to the person that does this.

Black said, "Everybody wants to know what's in it for them and especially if they're taking such a risk."

"I know," Q said. "What do you think is fair?"

"I don't know. She going to have to go on the trip?"

"No."

"Ten stacks."

Fresh said, "Wait a minute, you said she. Do you have someone in mind?"

"I do. I'm going to have to run it by them first."

"Run it by them, and then get back with me."

Black said, "So what's in it for me?"

"I'm going to make you a rich man. That's what's in it for you."

Black blew out a smoke ring. "That's exactly what I want to hear."

• • •

Todd and TeTe along with two big motherfuckers showed up at Dank's. He invited them in and offered them water and soda. They all sat in the living room of Dank's tiny apartment, which consisted of a flat screen, a coffee table and a pullout sofa. TeTe stood and studied Dank's face the whole time.

Finally he said, "I get that you're here because you want to know if I ran my mouth."

TeTe made her way over and stood in front of him. He wanted to pick her little tiny ass up and toss her out the window, but he knew if he did that, those two goons would surely kill his ass. The biggest one, named Country, had ashy rough cracked hands like he'd been picking cotton his whole life and Nate, the smaller of the two, was a big man as well. He looked to be about six foot four and around three hundred pounds. Dank himself was six foot three and about the same weight.

He couldn't believe Todd was there with them. Todd was his own flesh and blood and he was there on TeTe's side.

TeTe said, "No, I'm here to make sure that you don't think about running your goddamn mouth because if you do, the next time we show up here, it ain't gonna be good."

"Look, I'm sorry that I dropped the McDonald's bag and that's on me. I will go to trial on this. I haven't admitted to shit."

"Do you know how fuckin stupid this shits sounds? You dropping a goddamned McDonald's bag with the receipt in it."

Dank put his hand over his head and said, "I know. I know I fucked up, but I didn't say shit."

TeTe said, "What did your lawyer say?"

"I have a public defender. I was going to ask you if you could get me an attorney."

"Of course I will. I'll get you one of my attorneys."

Sweat beads rolled down his jaw and he turned to Todd, "You know I ain't going to say a motherfuckin' thang."

Todd shrugged his shoulders. Though Dank was his cousin, his loyalty was to TeTe. She paid his bills and she was right. This dumb-ass mistake could cost everybody their life.

TeTe said, "We have a total of four bodies. I'm not going down for your dumb ass. Do you understand me?"

Dank said, "Yes."

"Yes, what?"

"Yes, I understand."

The big ugly motherfucker named Country stood and walked over to Dank and placed his hands on his shoulder. "You will be addressing her as ma'am."

"Yes, ma'am."

TeTe made her way to the door. The three men trailed her pretty ass. Dank followed them until he reached the door.

Just before the door shut, TeTe said, "Remember what I said. Run your motherfuckin' mouth, I'll kill you."

"Yes." He tried to secure the door but Country stopped it with his alligator hands.

"Yes, what?"

"Yes, ma'am."

The door closed. Dank had been bitched and there was nothing he could do about it. While he didn't appreciate TeTe showing up at his house threatening him, he understood the nature of the business that they were in. He shouldn't take it personal but he did.

Chapter 14

WRAPPED IN SALMON COLORED DESIGNER SHEETS, BLACK SLAPPED Sasha's ass with his dick and it was turning her on. She turned and faced him, her smile revealed straight white teeth. Her hair pulled into a ponytail.

"I know we're supposed to be just business partners, but you make me feel so alive when I'm with you." Sasha said.

"Good. I'm glad cuz that's what I'm here for."

"What if I told you I wanted more?"

"That might be possible."

She smiled and said, "Are you serious?"

"I want to take you away from all this."

"What do you mean? We have our businesses and they're doing well."

"I'm talking about your father. I want to take you away from him."

"I would like that."

"I need your help though."

"You know I'll do anything for you."

"I need you to charter me a private plane."

"I've never done that before."

"You have an Amex, right?"

"Yes."

"That's all it takes."

"And what are you going to do with it?"

"Listen, don't worry about it. The less you know, the better off you'll be and that's real."

She smiled and leaned forward and kissed him. "I love you, Black. I know you don't love me, and you don't have to say that you love me, but I just thought I would tell you."

Black heard her but he didn't respond; instead, he slipped his dick inside her and yanked her hair hard and said, "Call me daddy, bitch!"

"Daddy, I love when you force me into submission. Can you tie me up tonight?"

• • •

Brooke came running back to Starr's office and said there was a man that wanted to see the owner. When Starr entered the studio, she saw one of the most handsome black men she'd ever seen in her life. He was about six foot five with skin the color of hot coco, a clean-shaven face and squinted eyes.

He extended his hand to Starr and said, "Is this your studio?"

"I'm the owner. How can I help you?"

The man never made eye contact with Starr; instead, he paced and surveyed the place over while nodding. Finally he turned and said, "Impressive. The name's Terrell."

"Thank you, Terrell, but I don't know exactly what you mean by that."

"Look, I've been looking all over Atlanta for a black company to work with but most of them have shabbily designed studios or they're just not professional. I love your studio and you seem very professional."

Starr smiled and said, "Thanks." All the while, thinking the last thing she needed to be dealing with was a cheap motherfucker that wanted a price break and Terrell fit that description. She'd seen it time and time again. Uppity-ass niggas coming in wearing designer clothes and driving expensive foreign cars while wanting her to give them the sun and the moon.

"Is there something I can do for you?"

"Actually there is."

Star stood there waiting while he continued to examine the place like he worked for Social Services. But she'd seen his type before. Wanting her to adhere to the highest levels of professionalism. Looking for something to scrutinize, but if she was a white establishment they wouldn't say a motherfuckin' thing.

"I'm moving into a new house and I'm going to need my house decorated."

Starr smiled. "You've come to the right place. How big is the house and what's the budget?"

"Well, the house is pretty big,"

"How big...Square footage?"

"I don't remember." Then he presented her a picture of the house on his iPhone. It was a mansion worth at least three million dollars.

"Very nice house."

He smiled and said, "Thanks. So, I'm looking for a deal."

She knew it. He was a rich motherfucker that had probably pulled himself out of the ghetto. Probably a former athlete and now he wanted a deal, but she wasn't going to sell herself short, regardless of how attractive he was.

"What kind of deal?"

"I don't know. I was thinking that you probably got your furniture wholesale, and maybe you could give me the wholesale price."

"Now why would I do that?"

"Because I'm giving business to you."

"Thank goodness for that. Because without your business I was going to get evicted. My car was going back and my son was going to get kicked out of private school." Starr said sarcastically to let his corny ass know that she would be okay without him.

He smiled. "Hey, I had to ask."

"Okay, you asked. All I can promise is my prices will be very reasonable."

They shook hands.

Chapter 15

SHAKUR'S BROTHERS ENTERED BIG PAPA'S HOME. HE THOUGHT about telling security not to let them come up, but hell, he didn't have anything to hide. He'd done what they'd asked him to do, so he let them inside. Rakeem and Jabril sat across from Big Papa who offered them water.

"We didn't come to drink. In fact, we didn't come to socialize."

Big Papa just stared at the tiny-ass Jabril and thought he could have smashed his ass back when he was in shape but those days were long gone. He could only hope for a thirty-second fistfight nowadays and even then, he knew that he'd be out of breath. And there were two of them and he spotted Jabril's gun print.

Big Papa said, "Look. I loved your brother and your brother loved me. We were like brothers."

Rakeem said, "My brother spoke highly of you, and he loved you too, man."

"I don't understand how I can help you avenge your brother's death. I already told you what I knew. I even called Jada over."

"We want Black."

"I don't know Black."

"I think you're lying."

"Never met Black."

"So you don't know Black?"

"No."

"You're from Atlanta?"

"I am, but I don't know everybody in Atlanta. That's impossible." Big Papa stood and walked to the kitchen, opened the fridge, grabbed a Diet Dr. Pepper and cocked his gun behind the fridge door. He didn't like the tone coming from Shakur's brother and he figured that if he was going to get shot, at least he would take one of them with him. He stuffed the .380 in his pocket.

When he came back in the living room, Rakeem was standing up and looking around the condo.

"Nice place you got here."

"Thanks."

"You must love it here."

"I do."

"Look, Ty. We don't want to cause you any problems. And nobody has to get hurt, you know what I mean?"

"Huh?"

"We need to find Black."

"I'm telling you I don't know nobody named Black. I swear to God."

"Call Jada."

"Are you out of you mind? After I tried to set her up?"

Big Papa thought he'd played this game with them long enough, and now it was time for him to call back up. He didn't have anybody in Atlanta that would help him. The truth was everybody thought he was soft and that's why he had Shakur as a friend. Shakur protected him and he provided Shakur with coke, but now that Shakur was gone, he needed protection. He would have to ask his connect to send some members of the Mexican Mafia to Atlanta to make sure he was okay.

"We need Jada or Black. Somebody has to pay for this. Understand, Ty?"

Both of the brothers made their way to the door and Big Papa followed them.

Before he let them out, Jabril turned and said, "Oh yeah, you'd do better if you used that gun in your pocket on yourself. You come out better because if you ever think about pulling that thing out on me, I'll kill you, fat boy."

•   •   •

Black arrived at his baby mama's house to see his kids. Black's kids, Man-Man and Tierany came running to Black and hugged him as soon as they laid eyes on him.

"Daddy!" Tierany said.

Black sat his crutches on the floor and scooped the little girl up and planted kisses all over her pretty little face. When he sat her down, she said, "You like my dress?" She wore a triple tier pink dress with white polka dots and a white belt. She spun around so he could take a good look.

"I love your dress, baby!" Black said, thinking his little girl was growing up and she was going to be a gorgeous young lady. Black knew there would be drama with the boys as soon as she was a teenager.

Tierany said, "We took school pictures today."

Man-Man had a striking resemblance to Black and this was a constant reminder of Asia and Black's rocky relationship. Black put his son in a headlock and said, "How you been, champ?"

"Good. Can you give me some money?"

"Money for what?"

"I want a new game for my PS4."

"How much is it?"

"Sixty-five dollars."

"You need a job."

Asia said, "Like you done ever had a job in your life. What the hell do you know about a job?"

Tierany said, "My daddy has his own business."

"That's right, baby," Black said.

Asia said, "Kids, go play. I wanna spend a couple of moments with your daddy."

When the kids were gone, Asia said, "Black, what the fuck have you done in my car?"

"What are you talking about?"

"Two detectives came by here yesterday saying that my car was seen leaving the scene of a triple murder."

"What? I don't believe that."

"Where the fuck is the car then, Black?"

"It's in the shop. I'm getting new tires. The radiator is getting replaced." Black lied.

"Black, why are you lying to me?"

"I ain't lying." There was an armchair on the other side of the room. Black sat himself down and Asia, still standing with her hands on her hips, wanted to slap the fuck out of him for lying to her face.

"So, what did you tell the detectives?"

"What the fuck do you mean, what did I tell the detectives? Why are you worried about it if you had nothing to do with it? And that is exactly how I know your black ass is lying."

"No, I just don't wanting them questioning you about some bullshit. Don't nobody have time for all of that."

"Black, what happened?"

"What did you tell them?"

"I told them somebody must have stolen the car. Led them to the back yard where the car was parked and of course, it was gone. I sounded surprised because I still have the key in my possession."

"Good."

"That is not good. If they find out I'm lying for you, I'm going to prison."

"You have nothing to worry about."

"I'm telling you right now, Black. If they catch you and find out that you're my kid's father, I'm telling everything that I know. I ain't going to jail for you or nobody else."

"Ain't nobody going to jail." Black stood and approached Asia. He tried to hug and console her but she shoved him away.

"Get the fuck out of my way. Get your motherfuckin' hands off me."

"You tripping."

"I'm tripping?"

"I paid for that car."

"It's in my name. Triple murder? What the fuck? You are nothing but the devil and you're going to get yours. I swear to you I believe what they say about you. I believe that you had Lani murdered."

Black placed his finger on the tip of her nose before Asia swatted it down. Tierany and Man-Man entered the room.

Man-Man said to Asia, "Why are you fussing at my daddy?"

"Fuck yo' Daddy!"

Tierany bear hugged Black's leg and Black gave her a kiss on the forehead before Asia wedged herself between Tierany and Black.

"Get out!" Asia said as she pointed toward the door.

"What? You gonna show me out like that in front of my kids?"

"Kids that you don't give a fuck about."

"I love all my kids. I do everything for all of my kids."

"Money ain't shit. What about time? What about showing your son how to be a man? Showing your daughter how to be treated by a man? You ever thought about that?"

Then Asia turned to the kids and said, "Go to your rooms right now!"

"You don't have to go nowhere." Black said.

"They do as long as they're under my roof." And she said to the kids again. "Go to your motherfuckin' room right now!"

The kids were walking toward their rooms when Black grabbed Tierany by the arm and said, "I'll take them with me."

Asia shoved Black in the back. "Get out right now! I'm calling the police and I'll tell them everything on your black ass. Try me, motherfucker!"

"It's like that now?"

"It's like that." Asia's hands rested on her hips.

She walked over toward the door and said, "Get out of here, Tyrann."

Black stood there for a moment. He wanted to beat the fuck out of Asia, but Man-Man and Tierany were standing there with rivers of tears rolling down their faces. He approached his kids and kissed them. He then left without incident.

Chapter 16

AFTER STARR VISITED TERRELL'S HOME, SHE KNEW THERE WAS NO way that she was going to let him tell her what she would pay. She decided that she would offer a slight discount on the furniture but what she had learned from these types of clients was that they were hard to please. The man's house was humongous. A huge Mediterranean-style home sitting on a half-acre behind the gates of a protected cul-de-sac. She and Terrell stood in his driveway facing a wooded area and went over the specifics of the agreement, the budget and what day she would get started.

Terrell said, "You sure you can't give me a discount?"

Starr just stared at this clown. Surely he was kidding. Here he was staying in this three million dollar mansion and driving a Maserati. He had to be kidding.

Starr said, "I want to live in a house like this one day and the only way I'm going to be able to do it is to be about my business."

Terrell laughed and said, "Well, you look like you're doing pretty good for yourself."

"I'm doing okay." Starr sighed then said, "Look, I'll give you a discount on the furniture but that's the best I can do."

"What kind of discount?"

"I get a fifty percent discount on all furnishings and I'll give you half of that."

He shook her hand and said, "Look, I don't want you to think I'm cheap."

Starr was already thinking the motherfucker was cheap, but she just nodded. Starr said, "So, what do you do?"

"I'm retired."

"Huh? You look too young to be retired."

"Well, I played in the NBA for ten years then I retired. I loved basketball but I knew there was more to do with life. So I retired at thirty. Now I'm starting a career in commercial real estate."

"Hmm, I'll have to ask my daddy if he has heard of you."

"Well, my NBA career wasn't that spectacular. If he's heard of me, it will probably be because of my college days."

"I'm sure he's heard of you. All he does is watch sports all day on the weekends."

There was an awkward silence and then Terrell said, "You don't have a ring."

"Huh?"

"You're not married."

"No." Starr smiled. She hated when people pointed that out and this had been a problem with a lot of clients. She'd bought a fake ring to wear sometimes because she noticed that when she wore the ring, it put a lot of the women at ease. Though she wasn't the type of woman that would go after another woman's man. She knew here in Atlanta that was a big deal.

"Why not?"

"Well I was engaged but my man got murdered."

"I'm sorry."

"It's okay."

"I'm divorced. Married the wrong woman."

"At least you found out while you were young."

Terrell stared at Starr curiously. "What do you mean?"

"Some people spend their whole life with the wrong person."

He smiled pensively and then said, "I suppose you're right."

"You're dating?"

"Yes, I have someone."

"I should have known. I mean, there is no way a gorgeous woman like you is going to stay single for long."

Starr blushed and said, "Thank you." She quickly changed the subject "When do you want me to start?"

"In two weeks. I will send you a check in the morning and then you can shop."

"Okay."

"Starr? I'm sorry, Ms. Coleman?"

"No, you can call me Starr."

"Do you think I'm cheap?"

"No," Starr wondered to herself why he gave a damn about what she thought.

"Oh, okay, because I'm not. I just grew up dirt poor and I worked so hard to pull myself up by my bootstraps and I don't want to go broke like so many other athletes. I don't want you to think I'm a nickel-and-dime-ass nigga."

Did he just say nigga? She was caught off guard but she was glad he'd said that. He was less stuffy than she thought. But she should have known. Most ghetto athletes are nothing but hood dudes that made it. Legit thugs is what her and her friends used to call them.

"Just being conservative?"

"Yes."

"I understand."

"Good because if you don't want to discount the furniture, I'll still work with you. Because from what I can see, you do quality work and you have to pay for quality."

"You do." Starr said. "I appreciate your confidence in me and I'm sure you're going to tell some of your NBA friends about me."

"I will."

Starr shook Terrell's hand and made her way back to the car. She could feel him looking at her ass.

Chapter 17

BLACK FOUND TWO DUFFEL BAGS FULL OF MONEY IN THE HOUSE when he walked in the bedroom. Stacks and stacks of money. When he went to the basement, he saw L giving Avant a haircut.

"L, you robbed somebody else?" Black said.

"What difference does it make?"

"You don't get it do you?"

L stood and he and Black were face to face. There was an awkward silence. Avant looked on, his hands bound by riot handcuffs. The sides of his head shaved. He wished he was dead. He hated Black but he despised L more. He wished that they would kill each other.

L said, "Have you forgotten that if it wasn't for me, you would be dead now?"

"What does that have to do with anything?"

"I'll do anything for you."

Black said, "Let's talk upstairs."

He made his way up to the top of the stairway. L trailed him and when they got to the top of the stairs, Black made eye contact with L.

"Look, man, I literally owe you my life...I do. I mean you saved my life and I will always be grateful for that."

L was silent. Truth was he wanted to smack the fuck out of Black for thinking that he was his daddy.

Black said, "You can do whatever the fuck you want to do. Just make sure don't nobody follow you back here. Is that understood?"

"Look, man. I'm good at what I do. If I wasn't, you wouldn't have hired me."

Black had to admit that L wasn't the brightest person in the world, but he was terrific at what he did.

"We can split the money."

"I don't want your money."

"I want you to take half. At least take half the money that I took from your homeboy. You deserve that. You were there."

Black knew he was right about that. Though he hated that three people had to die that day, he knew that he should receive half of that money.

"How much money do you have in all?"

"Close to three hundred thousand in cash and jewelry."

"Damn."

"I know, right?"

"Look, I just want you to be careful."

"I will, but what the fuck are we going to do with Avant. It's been over a month."

"Don't worry, we're going to kill him soon so don't get too attached."

"I can care less about Avant. Fuck him."

Black said, "No, that's your job."

L laughed his ass off and said, "Good one."

• • •

Jada was parked across from Big Papa's building so she could confront his fat ass and let him know that she knew he had tried to have her murdered. Three hours had passed since she first arrived, and she was about to leave when she spotted his Bentley leaving. She jumped right behind him in her rented Benz. She knew that he didn't recognize the car and he pulled over immediately and lowered his windows.

Jada parked her car and jumped out. They were now face-to-face. She didn't know why, but she didn't hate him. She felt disappointed and she wanted to know why? Why did he want her dead? Though she'd used him, she would never want anyone to harm him. She did care about him.

Big Papa said, "Hey."

Jada nervously kicked rocks in the parking lot and said, "Hey, Ty."

It was very awkward for them both. There was so much she wanted to say to him, but she just wanted to curse him the fuck out.

"Look, Jada, I'm sorry."

"Sorry?" Jada looked confused though she knew damn well what he was sorry for.

"Yeah. I'm sorry for what happened to you."

"What happened to me?"

"Don't play dumb."

"Why did you do me like that, Ty? What have I ever done to you?"

He parked the car and hopped out. They were face to face and both knew this would be the last time they ever spoke to one another. It was the first time she didn't view him as a trick and he didn't look at her as the sex kitten that she was. He totally ignored the tight jeans that gripped her ass so wonderfully. None of that mattered anymore. Nor would it ever matter again. Once someone thinks that you wanted them murdered, friendships are beyond repair.

"Jada, I didn't have a choice."

"So it had to be me, huh?"

"Jada, you're still here."

"I am." She pointed toward the sky.

"Look, they told me they were going to murder me and my family. My children."

"You believed them?"

"I did."

"Who are they?"

"Shakur's brothers, the Detroit dudes I was telling you about."

"They don't think I had something to do with it, do they?"

"They don't know who did. All they know is their brother is dead and some dude named Ty had a girlfriend that knew who did it."

"But I didn't know anything about it."

"I know you didn't."

"But why in the fuck did you have to be such a pussy? Why did you try to set me up? Why did you have me come to that IHOP? You knew that they were going to try to kill me, yet you let me walk outside and jump in the car."

He dropped his head. He couldn't stand to look at her. She was right and his conscience was screaming at him. What he had done was terrible. It was fucked up.

"But, you know what, Ty? God had bigger plans for me. It wasn't my time. God didn't want me to go."

"Look, I'm sorry."

"Fuck you."

Big Papa stood there looking stupid as hell.

"You wanted me dead. Final."

"I didn't want you dead. I just didn't want to die."

"So it was me or you, right, fat boy? I knew you were a bitch. That's why I could never get into you. I need a man, not a fuckin coward and you're a coward."

"It's not like that. I didn't want them to do anything to you."

"Whatever."

"Jada, they wanted to know where you live. I didn't tell them. I saw them a few days ago and they wanted me to tell them where you lived and I didn't."

"Only because you don't know where the fuck I live."

"Your address is 1313 Beach Tree Lane.

"How did you know that?"

"I followed you home one night. And I know about your little boyfriend—the one from Texas."

"What? You're a fuckin stalker!"

"I liked you, Jada. I loved you. I thought it would be me and you. I was stupid enough to believe that you actually wanted me. But I should have known you were too good to be true to me."

"So you wanted me dead?"

"I didn't want you dead. I'm telling you. They threatened to kill my family."

"I don't believe it. You have money. You have connections. You could have gotten somebody to protect you."

"Shakur was one of my best friends who just happened to be my muscle."

"I told you it was going to end bad. I warned Shakur."

"He didn't like Black, and he looked at it as backing down from Black."

"It didn't have to end like that."

"Jada, I'm sorry." He turned his back to her.

Jada hopped on his massive back and beat his head like he was a drum. He flung her little ass to the ground.

"Fuck you, fat boy! Fuck you!"

He got into his car. He was sorry for what he'd done to her. He knew he had really betrayed her. They made eye contact for the last time and Big Papa screeched away.

Jada got up and brushed herself off.

Chapter 18

FRESH WAS LYING ON HIS BED TRYING TO FIND SOMETHING TO WATCH on TV when he flicked the TV onto the local news. They were showing a picture of a Camaro highlighting the license plate. The newscast said that it was seen leaving the scene of a triple murder a week ago. Someone had recorded the car on their iPhone.

Fresh recognized the car immediately. It looked like the car that Black had been driving. He called him right away.

"Hello?" Black said.

"It's Fresh."

"What's up?"

"Come see me."

"Is it important?"

"Very important."

"You want me to come by your room?"

"No. Let's meet at Atlanta Bread Company in forty-five minutes."

"See you then."

Fresh sat in the back of the restaurant sipping lemonade when Black approached.

Black sat at the table and said, "What's up?"

"I want you to be honest with me."

"I will."

"They were showing a car on the news that was at the scene of a triple murder. Was that your car?"

"What kind of car?"

"Your Camaro."

Black sighed but maintained eye contact with Fresh.

"It was your car, wasn't it?"

"Look, it wasn't my fault. It was your fault. You gave me the bad dope, I tried to sell it and when Memphis found out it was fucked up, he was going to kill me."

"You told me that but what you didn't tell me is that you killed three people."

"We had to."

"I understand, but I can't do business with you, bruh. I can't. No way."

"Come on, man. You tripping."

"Black, it's just a matter of time before they get you. You don't get away with triple murder. Nobody does."

"If that's the way you feel."

"Even if I wanted to do business with you, Q is not going to go for it. I can tell you that now."

"But none of this would've happened if the coke was right."

"That's the way the chips fall sometimes."

Black pounded his fist hard on the table, and Fresh's drink spilled on the floor.

Fresh said, "Was that supposed to scare me?"

Black stood and said, "Not at all, my brother. I'm just pissed. I feel you and if you don't want to deal with me, I understand. I appreciate what you done for me."

Fresh offered his hand, and after a few seconds, Black shook.

"It's not personal, my nigga, it's business," Fresh said.

"For sho."

•   •   •

Butterfly opened the door and screamed, "Mama, your friend is here! The real black one!"

Black grinned at the little girl. He kneeled down and said, "Did you have fun at school today?"

"I don't go to school."

"What?"

"I'm home schooled. You know, when your teacher comes to your house and teach you?"

"Wow, must be nice."

"Not really. Can you give me some more money like you did the last time?"

TeTe was coming down the spiral staircase wearing a pantsuit and a Hermes belt. She yelled from the top of the staircase, "I didn't know you would be over so fast! I was getting dressed!" Her scent lingered in the air.

Butterfly had her hands out waiting on Black to present her with a hundred dollar bill.

TeTe said, "Butterfly, if you don't take your little ass back to your room..."

TeTe turned and faced Black. He embraced her and gripped her ass.

She pushed him back a little and said, "Was she begging for money?"

"No," Black lied.

"That jacket looks nice on you."

"Yeah, somebody special bought it for me."

"Is that so?"

"Yeah."

"A woman. A grown-ass woman."

TeTe laughed and then she led him upstairs to her bedroom. He sat on a chair in the corner across from the bed as she disappeared into a huge closet that contained over a thousand pairs of heels and over six hundred purses. Seconds later, she returned with two pairs of heels that were similar in style. One was Jimmy Choo and the other Prada.

She presented them to Black and said, "What should I wear?"

"They both look the same."

"You're such a man."

"You like that?"

"I do. Just so you know, they are similar, but they're not the same."

"What's the difference?"

"The Jimmy Choo is an inch higher."

"Well, that's the one I want you to wear."

"Why?"

"Elevates that ass. The way I like it."

"Ask a man something. Expect to get a man answer."

"I'm just telling you what I like."

"I don't have a big ass though. I don't even have hips."

"But it's round though."

She slid into the heels and then said, "Where are you taking me tonight?"

Black frowned.

"Come on, baby, don't get mad." TeTe said.

"I'm not mad."

"I got beautiful because I want to go out. You know I like to be wined and dined, baby." She twirled and said, "Look at me, baby. I'm beautiful."

And crazy as hell. Black thought. Black finally conceded and said, "Where do you wanna go?"

"I don't know." She paused and then said, "Don't you wanna show me off?"

"You're so complicated."

"Because I don't need a man don't mean I don't want to be treated like a woman." She sat on his lap and he held her neck. He kissed her passionately as his fingers unbuttoned her blouse, struggling to find her breasts.

She removed his hand and said, "You're making me hot."

"That's my job."

"I want to go out and then when we get back, you can fuck my brains out." She stood up from his lap then sat on the bed and pushed her boob back under her bra before buttoning her shirt.

Black said, "My connect cut me off."

"You owe them money?"

"I don't owe nobody shit."

"Hey, I was just asking."

"No, it's because I'm a different type of dude."

"I don't understand."

"When somebody does something to me. I get even."

"Don't we all?"

"Well, I thought so, but apparently they think that the police might be looking at me."

TeTe took a deep breath and said, "Well, there is something I have to tell you."

"What?"

"One of the guys I sent to get Mike dropped a McDonald's bag with a receipt in it at Mike's house. The police looked on the receipt and found out the time that he was at the McDonald's. They went back to the store and got the footage of him buying his food. They arrested his dumb ass."

"Damn."

"Don't worry about this. This ain't got shit to do with you."

"I'm not worried. Nobody knows me but...you."

"And I ain't going to say a goddamned thing. In fact, nobody is going to talk."

"How can you be sure?"

"I just got a gut feeling he ain't going to open his mouth," TeTe said. She didn't want to tell Black that she'd paid Dank a visit and warned him not to open his motherfuckin' mouth or else there would be consequences and repercussions.

"Anyway, you don't need to worry about your connect. I told you that you don't have to do that. I'll take care of you."

Black looked at her like she was an alien. "I'm not that kind of man. First of all, no woman is going to take care of me. That's not me. I've always got my own and I ain't bout to start laying around, letting a chick take care of me."

"I didn't mean it like that."

"How did you mean it?"

She sprang from the bed then plopped on his lap again and rubbed his chest. "What I meant, daddy, was that you could help me. We could be partners. I can show you another way."

"Let me give it some thought."

"And to put your mind at ease. I'm not trying to trick you into a relationship."

"I never said that. Where did that come from?" Black eyed her suspiciously.

"It's strictly business but with benefits," TeTe said.

"I'm going to think about it."

"Think about putting your dick inside me." She kicked off her heels and dropped her pants. She was standing there with yellow lace panties that contrasted against her skin beautifully.

"What about dinner?"

"I'm about to give it to you." She smiled.

Black laughed and said, "You're too much for me."

She removed her panties and said, "Am I now?"

Chapter 19

FRESH HAD CALLED JADA AND SAID THAT HE WANTED TO TAKE HER shopping for being hospitable to him and to show her that he really did appreciate her. He really didn't know what shopping with Jada entailed, but he soon found out. First, they'd gone to Lord and Taylor's then Louis Vuitton and then the Gucci store. When it was all said and done, Fresh had bought Jada three handbags.

She couldn't decide on what shoes to get so she'd ordered Bryan, the gay store clerk, to bring back the YSL's and a pair of Louboutin boots. She held the YSL's in her hand and her foot was inside one of the Louboutins.

"Which one do you like?" she asked Fresh.

"I don't care."

She made a sad face. Then she asked Bryan, who was wearing a pair of black skinny jeans that were tighter than the tightest jeans that Jada had ever worn.

Bryan said, "To tell you the truth, girl. I like the red bottoms. They have star power."

"Star power?" Fresh said.

Grinning-ass Bryan looked at Fresh like he would fuck him if he got an inkling of a hint that Fresh would reciprocate. Bryan said, "Star power means standing out. Shining, baby. Jada's a diamond. She needs to shine."

"That's right, Bryan." Jada said.

"Get the Louboutins." Bryan said.

Fresh was annoyed as hell. He couldn't believe that he'd spent four hours in the mall shopping. He said, "Get them both. I got shit I gotta do."

Bryan said, "I like him, girl. He's a boss that takes charge and money ain't a thang to him."

Jada was just grinning. She didn't want to say that Fresh didn't belong to her. For that moment, he did and that's all Bryan needed to know.

Bryan boxed up the shoes and placed them in a bag and made his way to the register. Jada followed him and Fresh was two steps behind. The total came to $2612.78. Fresh gave Bryan $2700 and told him to keep the change. Bryan gave Jada the receipt.

"Keep him, chile, keep him."

They all were laughing their asses off. Fresh was looking at Bryan's ass wondering what the fuck happened to him. Walking around with a full beard wearing high-heeled shoes. Was he gay? Was he straight? Was he a tranny? This was something that he knew that he would have to get used to in Atlanta. Though there were certainly plenty of gay men in Houston, the Atlanta gay men were flaming. Especially the black ones. I guess that was what he meant by standing out.

Bryan passed Jada the bags and strutted his skinny ass to the front of the cash register. He glanced at Fresh's package on the low because Fresh certainly looked like the kind of dude that would beat the fuck out him if he knew that he was looking at him in that way. And he knew Jada was crazy.

Bryan hugged and kissed Jada and said, "Tootles, bitch."

"Thank you, Ms. Bryan."

"Girl, call me. You've been saying we gonna hang out forever."

"I'll call you."

When Jada and Fresh left the store, Fresh noticed a man staring at Jada. He said, "Hey, there is a man to your left staring at you. Do you know him?"

Jada glanced at the man. He did look familiar but she couldn't remember where she knew him from. Perhaps she had gone to school with him. "I don't know him."

"Jada!" the man called out.

Jada looked at the clown-ass nigga. His pants were sagging and he looked like he was damn near forty though he probably wasn't. She could tell that he'd probably lived a rough life.

"You know me?" she asked.

"Come on, how you gone play me like that?"

Jada stared at his silly ass. She knew that she hadn't fucked him, though she didn't know where she knew him from. The motherfucker looked like he didn't have thirty dollars to his name. Dusty-ass Levi jeans and old-ass, scuffed up Air Jordan's. If she'd fucked him, it was probably before she was fifteen.

"I'm Hunch."

"Hunch! Oh, how you been?"

"I'm good. Look like you doing good." Then he cut his eyes to Fresh.

"How is Tangie?"

"She's good. You talk to Mari?"

"No, but I'm going to see him."

"Okay, he calls Tangie all the time. She went to see him last week."

"Okay, Hunch, I gotta be going." Jada hugged him.

"Aight, Jada. Good seeing you." He stared at Fresh again like he was waiting for an introduction but it was too awkward for Jada. There was no way she was going to introduce Fresh to Hunch.

When Jada stepped away from Hunch, Fresh said, "Who was that?"

"Shamari's brother-in-law. Well, not his brother-in-law, but some lame-ass nigga that lives off Shamari's sister."

"Oh, okay. So he's going to probably report back to Shamari."

"Yes. Who gives a fuck?"

"I know I don't."

Chapter 20

L UNFASTENED THE CAGE AND DRAGGED AVANT OUT AND LOCKED lips with him. Avant resisted and positioned his head away from L's wet sloppy lips. L gripped his throat and shoved his tongue in the man's mouth. His hands went around Avant's waist and finally gripped his ass.

L whispered, "I want some of that sweet ass."

Avant frowned, but he didn't want to get L too mad. Yesterday, L had proclaimed his love for Avant and tried to make Avant say that he loved him back. Avant wouldn't say it and L beat him with a whip and bruised his ass cheeks. He kept beating him violently until Avant said that he loved him. Then L had raped him and made Avant call him daddy.

L released him from his grip and said, "Tell me you love me."

"I love you, daddy."

Avant was clearly a broken man and L was a broken soul. L passed him a bottle of baby oil.

"I want you to rub this on your ass cheeks. You know I like it when your ass cheeks are shining." L said.

"Anything for you, Daddy."

L smiled and said, "Give me another kiss."

L opened the cage and Avant crawled back inside.

L said, "Be good to me and I'll have a surprise for you."

Avant was sitting on the floor on a dirty-ass blue blanket applying baby oil to his ashy-ass legs. He said, "I would like that."

L smiled and was about to walk up to the top of the stairs before doubling back to lock the cage.

"Can you turn the light on for me?" Avant asked.

L hit the light switch and was halfway upstairs when Avant said, "Daddy." And as soon as he said it, he felt like a bitch. But this was the relationship that he and L had. He hated it, but it was his reality now. He was L's bitch.

"I'll be right down. Hold up." L sprinted to the top of the stairs and disappeared inside the kitchen and retrieved an eight-piece box of extra crispy KFC with mashed potatoes and gravy, coleslaw and sweet tea. He would reward Avant if he pleased him, but he knew that he would have to get rid the evidence before hating-ass Black came back.

L made his way back down the stairs carrying the box of chicken and a couple of paper plates. "After we make love, we'll have movie night."

Avant forced a smile.

L set the food on a table beside the cage near the television then, he said, "You were going to tell me something?"

"I have a cousin in Decatur."

"What about him?"

"He's loaded. More money than anybody I turned you on to in the past."

"Tell me more."

"He's the loud, man. He grows the shit. He got houses all over the city. When I tell you this dude is loaded, I ain't lying."

"What do you mean?"

"He has millions. He has a new Porsche Panamera"

"I don't give a fuck about cars."

"But you can get him."

"Why are you telling me this?"

"Because he has change-your-life money."

"Oh, yeah?"

"Yeah, I want to give you the information if you let me go."

"You know I ain't doing that."

"Look, if you have a compassionate bone in your body, you would let me go. Man, this ain't right."

L opened the cage and pulled his gun from his waist and cocked the gun. "A motherfucker like you don't tell me what the fuck to do." The cold steel pressed against Avant's face. "I will kill you, nigga!"

"Come on, man. Don't do it!" Avant pleaded.

L slapped the fuck out of Avant with the gun. Blood shot from Avant's mouth and nose and he toppled back. His bare stomach touching the cold floor. L ripped Avant's white lace panties down. Avant's shiny ass cheeks delighted L. L's penis was hard and ready, but he wanted to teach Avant a lesson. He wanted to let Avant know that L called the motherfuckin' shots and not Avant. L stood over Avant and the gun now pointed at his eye.

He said, "Where the fuck does your cousin live?"

"I dunno."

L slapped him again. This time he fired the gun and Avant screamed. He thought he'd been hit.

There was a broom lying on the other side of the room next to some cleaning supplies. L grabbed the broom and said. "Now, where does this cousin live or I'm raping your ass with this broom.

"He has a house in Decatur Heights. I don't know the address but I know the street name and what side of the road the house is on. You'll be able to tell it by the exotic cars in the driveway."

"Now, that's more like it." L said grinning. He stepped outside the cage, grabbed a chicken breast then reentered the cage pointing the gun at Avant's temple with the other hand. "Open your mouth. Daddy's got something for you."

Avant wanted to cry and he was still hanging on to the possibility of being set free to be with his children so he obliged. L chomped a drumstick while receiving oral from Avant.

Black and TeTe were in the Waffle House on Piedmont Avenue when someone tapped Black on the shoulder and said, "I know you."

At first, Black thought it was a woman, but when he looked closer, it was a damn tranny.

Black said, "Nah, you don't know me."

"What the fuck is going on, Black? Why did he say he knows you?" TeTe asked.

The tranny said, "You will refer to me as misses."

"What the fuck ever."

"You don't know me, partna."

"You are Larry's friend."

"Who?"

"You call him L. Remember that day in the park when you stopped him from choking me."

Black laughed and said, "Oh yeah."

TeTe relaxed when she realized that Black knew the tranny through somebody else.

Black said, "Oh yeah, you're—"

"Fy-head...Cassandra."

TeTe said, "Well, Cassandra, we're trying to have breakfast."

Fy-head stared at TeTe like he wanted to curse her the fuck out; instead, he just ignored TeTe's ass. "When is the last time you saw L?"

"A couple of days ago. Why?"

"Well, because I wanted to see if you can talk some sense into him."

Black said, "Have a seat."

TeTe came to Black's side of the booth and Fy-head sat across from them. Black said, "So what are you talking about?"

"You know Larry was institutionalized and he don't know how things work in the real world because he's spent most of his life in prison."

Black was listening but he really wanted to tell her to get to the point.

There was a cup of water on the table and Fy-Head said, "Can I have this water?"

"Help yourself." Black said.

Fy-head sipped the water through a straw and said, "L put his whole life on Facebook."

"I didn't know he had a Facebook page."

"Yes, he just recently got one. His niece made it for him, and I knew that was a big mistake because, like I said, Larry don't think like a normal person. He is sweet as can be but he just don't make rational decisions."

TeTe said, "Who the fuck is Larry?"

"I'll tell you later, babe."

"Can I have some of this bacon?" Fy-head asked.

"You can if you get to the point." Black said.

"Larry and I are seeing each other."

Black looked surprised. "You are?"

"Yeah, after that day when we were in the park, he had his niece find me on Facebook. We met up and he apologized. Then we made love."

"That's entirely too much information," Black said. Then he thought about the day that he'd walked in on L smashing Avant's ass cheeks to smithereens.

"Well, anyways. I wanted to know where Larry is getting all this money from. Every day, he is posting pictures of bags of money on Facebook, and one day, he even posted a pic of a gun. I told his stupid ass to take it down."

"Did he?"

"Yes."

Fy-head sipped the water and ate more bacon and said, "I dunno if you're dealing with him or not, but you should stay away from him because he's going to cause somebody to go to prison. Just the other day, he updated his status and said he had to slay three niggas."

"What did he mean by that?"

"I don't know, but you know Larry like I know Larry. One thing is for sure, he plays for keeps." Fy-head was smacking on the bacon like he hadn't eaten in days. "I asked him about the status and he said it was none of my business."

"Really?"

Fy-Head stood and said to TeTe, "I'm so sorry for interrupting your meal, but Larry is my friend and I don't want him to get into any trouble."

TeTe nodded and said, "It's okay." She examined Fy-Head's body and decided that it was so curvaceous that it would put most women's bodies to shame. She then said, "Cassandra, have you ever thought about making any extra money?"

"A bitch always need money. Doing what?"

"Taking men out."

"Tricking?"

"Well, if that's what you want to call it."

"That's what it is. I don't do that no more, boo boo."

"And why not?"

"HIV positive."

Black said, "What? Have a seat."

Fy-Head sat back down and Black said, "You are HIV positive?"

"Yes."

"Does L know?"

"Yes. I tell everybody that I have sex with. I don't play games. I'm very honest."

"Damn," Black said as he shook his head disgusted.

"Miss TeTe, I don't trick anymore, but if you have a card, I can pass it on to my friend Porsha. She will reach out to you if she's interested."

"How does she look?"

"Just put it this way. We call the bitch, Miss America."

They were laughing their asses off. Fy-head stood and then shook Black and TeTe's hands before making her way out of the door.

Chapter 21

SHAMARI DIDN'T HUG JADA WHEN HE CAME TO THE TABLE FOR visitation. She offered to hug him but he refused. There was an awkward silence between the two of them as he stared at her. She watched and wondered what the fuck was his problem.

She finally said, "So, if you're not going to talk. I'm going to take my ass home. Obviously you're not happy to see me."

"Should I be?"

"What?" Was this nigga out of his mind? Did he really think that she was obligated to come see him? Like she didn't have better shit to do.

"I took the rap for you, Jada, and this is the thanks I get?"

"What are you talking about? You took the rap for me? Nigga, I was never a drug dealer. You didn't take the rap for me. You did what you were supposed to do."

"I turned myself in, so you can be free after they caught you."

Jada wanted to curse the motherfucker out. She wanted to get loud, but she had to remember that she was in a prison visitation room and not a parking lot.

Shamari rested his elbows on the table. "You know how many motherfuckers would have let you go to prison?"

"Where is all this coming from?"

"I think you know."

Jada leaned forward and said, "You turned yourself in but have you forgotten that it was your shit, and I was the one trying to warn yo dumb ass that you were dealing with an informant. Have you forgotten that I basically sold ass to pay for your attorneys. I may not have been the most faithful, but you'd be hard pressed to find someone more loyal."

A few minutes of silence passed before Shamari said, "I'm sorry I'm tripping. It's rough in here, man. I want to get out of his motherfucker so bad."

Jada stared at him and she empathized for him. He had to spend the rest of his life behind bars and he was so young. He didn't deserve the sentence he got, but there was nothing either of them could do about it.

Tears cascaded down her jaw. "I wish there was something I could do to get you out. You know that I would do it."

"Don't cry, baby. I'll be alright. I just had a moment."

Jada removed some tissue for her face and dabbed her eyes.

"I spoke to Hunch."

"I know."

"He told me that he'd seen you with some guy in the mall."

"I knew he would tell you, but I don't know why he would tell you."

"He said you were acting strange."

"I didn't recognize him.

"Who is he, Jada?"

"Just a friend of mine."

"Is he your new boyfriend?"

"No."

"Hunch said he was dark skinned and he sounded very much like Black."

"It's not?"

"You sure?"

"Hell, yeah! This guy is from Texas, someone that Trey knew."

"Black would do something like that."

"Like what?"

"Talk to my ex."

"I can assure you, it's not Black."

Another awkward silence, then Jada said, "It's not going to change anything between us, Shamari. I will still come see you and still send you money and he knows about you."

"You know I wanna flip this goddamned table, don't you?"

"Why?"

"It hurts."

"I know it does, but I'm glad it's out in the open."

Shamari sighed and said, "I guess that's a good thing."

Jada and Shamari talked for the next twenty minutes mostly about their families and then Jada announced that it was time to go.

"Is he waiting?"

"No, I have to take Louise to the thrift store. You know how my mama loves the thrift stores."

"So do you."

"I didn't have a choice. I grew up wearing thrift-store stuff, and besides, you can find some good stuff in there. Ain't nothing wrong with thrift stores."

"I didn't say there was," Shamari said. "That's just something that I know about you. You know, I know everything about you and you know everything about me. I know stuff that he doesn't know about you."

"Who doesn't know about me?"

"Your new man."

"You do know me better than anybody."

"That'll never change."

She smiled and felt awkward talking to him. She glanced at her watch.

"I know you gotta go. Leave old Shamari behind the wall," he said.

"I suppose I can stay for a few more minutes. Louise can wait."

He was smiling and admiring her beauty at the same time, and he said, "You smell so damn good."

"Bond No. 9. Madison Square Park." Fresh had bought it for her and he loved it so she wore it.

"You hate Bond No. 9."

"I found one that I like."

"I wish I could rip your clothes off. But I know he wouldn't like that."

"You're crazy, boy."

"I like when you call me a boy although I'm a grown man."

"You'll always be a boy to me. I met you when you were a boy."

"Do you remember the first time we met?"

"Of course I do. We were at the skating rink. I think we were seventeen."

"Yeah, and you told me you didn't like light guys."

"I did tell you that." She laughed "And I didn't."

"But I changed that."

"You did."

"But you can't wait for me?"

"What do you want me to do? Stop my life? You have life."

"You're right, baby. I can't be that selfish."

They both stood and he hugged her. He whispered in her ear, "You sure it's not Black?"

Chapter 22

STARR HAD WRAPPED UP DECORATING TERRELL'S HOUSE WITH THE help of her assistant for the day, T.J. He had been a tremendous help to her except for when he'd let go of a lamp and it shattered into pieces, luckily it wasn't an expensive item. She wanted to be angry with him, but when he said, "I'm sorry, Mommy" with his cute little face, it was hard to be angry with him. Particularly, since she loved when he called her mommy.

She just fussed a little bit and warned him to pay attention. She told him that if he broke anything else, it was coming out of his pay. He'd wanted a video game that cost about sixty bucks and she had promised that if he helped, she would get the game for him and so far he'd been fantastic. Terrell had been in Seattle on a business trip and as soon as he got back, he headed home and Starr was still there decorating although she was almost finished.

T.J. approached Terrell before he even had a chance to enter the house and said, "I'm sorry. I didn't mean to break your lamp."

Terrell gazed at Starr as if he wanted to say what in the hell is he talking about.

Starr said, "I'll explain."

Terrell kneeled and said, "You know what that means, my man. You broke my lamp that means that I'm going to have to call the police on you."

"No! Mommy said she was going to pay for it."

"You're going to jail."

There was fear in T.J's face. The poor baby wanted to cry, but Starr came to the rescue and said, "Nobody is going to take my pooh bear to jail."

Terrell rubbed his hair and said, "You're so lucky that you have such a cute mommy. So I'm not going to call the police on you. This time."

T.J. grinned again.

He was smiling brightly when he entered the house. The place looked amazing. Starr had taken a conservative approach and decorated it with a manlier vibe, and it was sophisticated and warm with lots of browns, greys and earthy tones. He strolled through each room and he was even more impressed until he reached his man cave. The man cave had pictures made of old style wood, a leather sofa, bar with a sink and a faucet, a fridge and, of course, a Foosball machine. Terrell absolutely loved it until he saw a TV that he didn't order.

"What is that?"

"Umm...a television."

"I have televisions."

"They're antiquated."

"What are you trying to say?"

"I'm saying that if you're going to spend this much money, you might as well get the latest television." She powered the television up and turned it on to Sports Center. Highlights from the Atlanta Falcons were playing.

Terrell said, "Damn this picture is amazing."

"I thought you would like it."

"How much did it cost?"

"Six thousand dollars."

"What?"

"I bought it with my credit card. If you don't want it, I will take it back. You have to have this TV for this house. I mean really? How are you going to have a house like this with a K-Mart television? You have to treat yourself. Keep it for a week and if you still feel this way, I'll take it back."

He sighed then glanced at the television again. "I've never seen a TV like this in my life."

"It's time to start living."

"I guess you're right."

Starr said, "Do you mind if I take some pictures for my portfolio?"

"I don't mind at all."

Chapter 23

BLACK YELLED AT L. "WHAT ARE YOU, FUCKING NUTS?"

L just stood there looking stupid, wondering what the fuck Black was complaining about now. Always bitching. Always thinking that he was his dad. Always trying to tell him what the fuck to do and he had just about had enough of this motherfucker.

Black said, "Why are you posting pictures on Facebook? Pictures of money and shit. Do you want to go back to prison?"

"Who told you that?"

"Is it true? I ran into your little friend today, and he told me your dumb ass is putting up status updates saying that you just knocked off three busters and stupid shit like that."

"You ain't my motherfuckin' dad and I'm about tired of your shit. You hear me," L said pointing at Black. "I don't need you to tell me what the fuck to do."

"So it's true. You have been posting dumb shit on Facebook. I didn't even know your ass had a Facebook account."

"What's wrong with having a Facebook account? Everybody has a Facebook account."

"That don't mean that you need to have one."

"Give me one reason I don't need to have an account!" Then L said, "Fuck it, I ain't got to explain shit to you. I'm going to get the fuck out of here today. You don't have to worry about me. Just pay me what you owe me and I'm out."

Black disappeared into his room and went into his safe. He came back out and gave L twenty grand.

"See! I do all the hard work and you give me this bullshit."

"What do you think you deserve?"

"Look, this is the exact reason that I do what I do."

"What is it that you do?"

"I take mine because of motherfuckers like you that don't want nobody else to shine."

"Look, L, take the money and get the fuck out of here. When I come back home, I want you gone. Leave my keys under the mat." Black was walking toward the door then he turned around and said, "One more thing. How can you fuck a man that you know is HIV positive?"

"What I do is my business."

"You don't care if you die?"

"I'll take my chances. We're all gonna die."

"What about your baby and your baby mama?"

"Both are negative since you want to be all concerned and shit."

"What about you? Are you HIV positive?"

"Now this is what I don't understand. How can you judge me when you're just as bad as me? Black, we ain't no angels. We both are going to have to plead our case to get into heaven."

"But see, the difference between me and you is that I don't do shit to people I care about. I don't put them at risk."

"Are you fucking serious? Nigga, you are the reason Lani is dead right now."

"You didn't know Lani and you don't know what the fuck you're talking about!"

"You ain't no better than me. So don't judge me by what the fuck I do. One thing about me; if I like you, I'm loyal to you."

Black continued to the door and stopped. "Please be gone by the time I come back. Just do me that favor and get the fuck out. Will you?"

"I'll be gone, nigga."

•   •   •

Black was on his way to Nana's house when his phone rang. Private number. He answered it. It was a call from Shamari. He heard the prison recording and answered it immediately.

"Hello?"

"What's up, bruh?"

"Hey, I want to ask you a question and I want you to be honest with me."

"Ask me anything, man, but you know these calls are being recorded."

"It's nothing like that."

Black pulled over in a gas station parking lot. His intuition was telling him that this conversation was going to be a deep one for some reason.

Shamari said, "Are you fucking, Jada?"

There was a long pause and Black wondered why in the hell was Shamari asking him that. Though he knew exactly who Jada was fucking, there was no way he would tell Shamari. He had a relationship with Jada and she was a good person, and there was no way he was going to expose her.

Shamari said, "Are you still there?"

"Yes."

"Answer the question."

"Look, you know the answer to that question."

"I don't know the answer to that question. That's exactly why I'm asking you."

"I would never do that to you, bruh. That's my word."

"My brother-in-law said that he saw Jada in Phipps with someone that sounded like you."

"Did you ask Jada about it? Ask her who it was?"

"She told me she had a man but wouldn't reveal who it was. Do you know who he is?"

"I don't."

"But it ain't you?"

"No way, no how."

"Ok." There was an awkward silence.

"You don't believe me do you?"

"Why do you say that?"

"You don't sound like you believe me, and you've seen me do some dirty shit."

"I have."

"But I swear to you, bruh. I haven't ever fucked Jada. Would I fuck her if I wasn't your friend? Hell yeah, but I didn't do it to you, man."

"Ok, I'll take your word for it."

"What else is going on?"

"That's about it, and anyway, that's all I wanted. I have to go. It's almost count time."

"Okay, keep your head up and let me know if you need anything."

"For sure."

***•   •   •

Black entered Sasha's house again and he heard sounds of sex coming from her bedroom. He placed his ear to the door and he heard Sasha whimper as if she wanted to cry and a man's voice. Her father. The respected mayor of the city of Atlanta. A rapist, a molester and a pedophile.

Black could hear the mayor talking. "I want you to tell me you love me and there'll never be a man like me."

Black could hear her between breaths do as she was told. "I love you, Daddy, and there will never be a man like you."

"I want you to get on your knees and take me in your mouth."

Black was fuming. His hand was on his gun. He wanted to kick the motherfuckin' door in and shoot this perverted motherfucker in his head.

He could hear her giving him oral sex. Sloppy, disgusting sex and Black wondered how it got to this point for this man. He'd always heard that this was the type of shit that white people did. Not black people but he was hearing it.

He cocked his gun and he heard the mayor say, "Did I hear something?"

Sasha said, "Just probably the people upstairs."

"You right, now continue."

Black had made up his mind. He would count to three and kick the door in and blow this motherfucker's head off. He had to do it. There was no way that he could let his friend continue to suffer this kind of abuse. It was sick. It was disgusting and perverted. Black began to count.

His cell phone rang.

The mayor stopped and Sasha said, "That was my phone. It's on the kitchen counter."

Black decided to leave. He placed his gun back on his waist and exited the condo.

Chapter 24

DANK PHONED TODD AND TOLD HIM THAT A DETECTIVE HAD BEEN BY to visit him and that he needed to speak with TeTe right away. Two hours later, Todd showed up at Dank's small apartment along with TeTe who was holding a latte from Starbucks in her hand. She was wearing a pencil skirt and when her legs crossed, she revealed beautiful brown legs.

She said, "So, tell me what's up."

"A detective came by. Said that he wanted to talk to me."

"And did you invite him in?" TeTe asked. She nursed that latte and studied his face trying to get an idea if he was lying or not.

"I did. I wanted to know what he knew."

'What did you find out?

"He wanted to know about the other two men.

"He did?"

"He said that the phone records indicate that Mike was the last person that these two people spoke to and they are missing."

"No way a police officer told you all that."

"He did, and I think he was just letting me know that it was just a matter of time before he charged me."

"But why would he tell you all that?"

"He wanted me to help. Wanted me to tell him who was with me when I killed Mike."

"You admitted to killing Mike?"

"No, I didn't admit to anything. If they have no body, they have no murder."

"Exactly."

TeTe stood and paced while sipping her latte and thinking about what to do. "It's just a matter of time before they piece Shakur's murder together too."

"That's what I was thinking," Todd said.

"We gotta get you out of here. I want to send you away. You have to run."

Dank said, "Run?"

"Yeah, run. He has no choice."

Todd said, "Yeah, I gotta get the fuck out of here or else they're going to try to pin three bodies on me. I don't want to go to prison for the rest of my life."

"I have cousins in Chicago. We'll send you to chill up there. We gotta get you the fuck out of here." TeTe said.

She made her way toward the door and stopped when she reached the door. When she looked back, they were both still seated and she said, "What the fuck are you two waiting on? Get up and come with me."

Todd said, "I have this monitor around my leg."

TeTe scanned her purse, looking for the pocketknife that she always carried along with her handgun. The knife had a pink handle and she'd used it to carve a couple of bitches' faces up. When she found the knife, she ordered Todd to bring his ass over. She cut the monitor off and said, "You have five minutes to get your shit. We gotta get the fuck out of here now."

"How am I going to get to Chicago?"

"I will have someone drive you, don't worry. Just get your shit and leave the house arrest bracelet so by the time they realize that you're gone, it will be too late."

**•   •   •

Brooke banged on Starr's office door and informed her that Q was out front and wanted to see her. Star applied some lip gloss before heading out to the studio. She saw Q using her iPad to look at her portfolio. She eased up on him and startled him.

"Did I scare you?"

"Nobody scares me." He smiled.

"Except for me." She laughed.

He kept flipping through the pages admiring her designs. Her art. Her taste. She wasn't just a contemporary designer. She truly had an eye for design and it was obvious through her portfolio that she would cater to her customer's needs.

"Damn you're good," he said.

"You didn't think I was?"

"I didn't know."

"You've seen my home."

"Once. I should have let you do my condo."

"You didn't think I was good enough."

"No, it's not that. I didn't know. Now I know."

Starr said, "Let me show you my latest client's home.

Starr presented Terrell's house and Q was impressed with the size of the house. Then the first thing he noticed was the television.

"There's a TV like mine."

"I know."

"You stealing ideas from me?"

"Maybe."

He continued flipping through the portfolio until he came across a picture of T.J. and some strange man posing in the driveway of the house.

"Who is this guy?" he asked.

"The owner of the house."

"Damn. What does he do for a living?"

"Former athlete."

"Did he hit on you?"

"It was strictly business." She smiled and then said, "You getting jealous babe?"

"Maybe." He paused then said, "I don't want you to have customers like that."

"Like what?"

"Young, rich black men."

"This is Atlanta, baby. That's what it's like here." Then she said, "You are jealous."

"Maybe a little over the fact that he gets to play with T.J. and I don't."

Starr knew that he was earnest, and that he did want to be a part of T.J.'s life because he'd said it many times before.

"I want you to see T.J."

Starr glanced over her shoulder and noticed Brooke texting someone on her phone. She said, "Brooke, can you excuse us for a moment? As a matter of fact, take your lunch. You haven't had lunch, have you?"

Brooke glanced at her watch and said, "I'll be back in an hour. If you need me, call me."

When Brooke exited the showroom, Q said, "Why can't I see T.J.?"

Starr sighed.

"He's my godson. The boy needs a man in his life."

"I wanna let you see him, but—"

"But, what? What do you think I'm going to do? Take him along with me on a drug deal?"

"The boy has lost so many people, so early. I don't want somebody that's going to be in his life temporarily."

"I'm his godfather. What are you talking about? Trey was like my brother and whether me and you work out or not, I want him to know me. To know that he has a real man in his corner."

Starr knew he was right. Though T.J. spent time with her father, it was not the same. Her father didn't have the energy to do a lot of the things that T.J. wanted to do.

"You can see T.J."

Q smiled and said, "So when do I get to meet your family?"

"Whoa."

"I'm serious. I want to meet your mom. Your father. Your sister. I want to meet everyone."

"Let me think about that one, but first let's spend time with T.J."

"So have you officially adopted T.J. yet?"

"Not yet, just waiting to hear back from the courts but the adoption should go through any day now. He already calls me mommy and that makes me feel so good."

"We need to get T.J. a brother or sister."

"Is that so?"

"Yeah, it's lonely in this world."

She blushed, thinking that she would love to have his child, but he still needed to prove himself.

Fifteen minutes after Big Papa left his mama's house in Decatur, he noticed a silver Saab and an older, black Toyota 4runner trailing him. He made a right turn into a residential community and the Saab and 4runner still followed. He accelerated as fast as he could, hoping to see someone out in the community, perhaps pulling their trash to the edge of the street or walking their dog. He would turn in their driveway and strike up a conversation. Surely if they were after him, they wouldn't hurt him in front of innocent bystanders.

It was nine p.m. and he saw nobody until he turned a corner and spotted a person wearing a neon tracksuit jogging with a jogging light around his head. He slowed down. He would ask the man for directions and converse for a moment until his followers passed by. When he decelerated as he approached the jogger, the 4runner accelerated until it was parallel to him. They didn't give a damn about the jogger.

Big Papa reached for his weapon, but it was too late. A man dangling from the backseat window of the 4runner fired fifteen shots into the passenger door of Big Papa's Bentley. Two bullets entered Papa's skull and another one ripped into his chest. Papa's foot pressed the gas pedal and he crashed into a telephone pole. His foot still locked on the gas pedal caused the Bentley to toss up dirt and grass. Papa's head was slumped over the wheel and the jogger, who'd witnessed the whole thing, had his cell phone in his hand and was attempting to dial 911. Before he could dial the numbers, a dreadlocked man wearing a black hoodie and skinny jeans and red Air Yeezy's hopped out of the silver Saab and gunned his ass down immediately. His cell phone crashed to the sidewalk shattering the iPhone screen and blood drenched his Nike running shirt. He'd obviously picked the wrong time to go jogging. The shooter ran, gripping his sagging pants with one hand before catching up with the Saab. Then the man jumped into the Saab and the two vehicles raced out of the neighborhood.

Chapter 25

TETE TEXTED BLACK AND TOLD HIM THAT FY-HEAD HAD BEEN TRYING to get in touch with him. Saying that it was very important that he call him and it was about L. Black called Fy-Head right away.

"Hello?"

"Yeah I just called to tell you about Larry's latest status update on Facebook."

"I don't fuck with L no more. We're not friends. He wants to do things his way and I want to do things my way."

"I figured that much cuz he called me cursing me out. Telling me that I wasn't shit. Wondering why I told y'all that I was HIV positive. I tried to explain to him that I just didn't volunteer that information. I was asked by your girlfriend if I wanted to turn some tricks and I explained to her why that wouldn't be an option. But he went off. Called me all kinds of sluts and accused me of giving him HIV. I did give it to him, but I always told Larry that I was HIV. I don't play games. Playing games will get you killed. You remember the girl I was with at the park that day when Larry choked me?"

Black wanted to say he didn't remember nor did he give a fuck, but said, "I vaguely remember."

"Well, she had met this dude on Tinder."

"What is Tinder?"

"It's a dating app."

"Okay."

"Yeah, she had met this dude on Tinder and had him fooled into thinking she had been born a woman. When he found out that she had been born a man, he beat the fuck out of her with a baseball bat. Broke her jaw, broke her ribs. Now the bitch is laying up in AMC sipping soup through a straw, but I told her, don't play those kind of games with no grown-ass man."

"What does this have to do with anything?"

"I'm sorry. I know I can get carried away."

"Yeah, but I don't fuck with L no more."

"But I'm just worried about him. His last status update said, 'Get rich or die trying.' "

"L is a grown man."

"Can you talk to him?"

"I've done all the talking I can."

"I know, chile. He so damn hard-headed. I called him and asked him what that status meant. He said it meant exactly what it meant. That somebody had something that belonged to him and that he planned to get it."

Black thought about the day that L had murdered three people for him and though he and L wasn't on good terms, he wanted to call him and tell him to come back to the house. L had proven to be loyal to him and that loyalty had been hard to find. Impossible to find.

"Look, I'll call him."

"Thank you."

"I'm just curious. Why do you care about L so much?"

"Larry is a good person. He's like a big old teddy bear, but he's lost his way out here. He talks about you all the time. I mean he really don't like letting you down. He says that you're the only person that has ever done anything for him. He cares about what you think of him."

"He don't act like it."

"You know how Larry can be. Stubborn as hell."

"Yeah, he's a good dude, overall. I mean he has some issues, but don't we all."

"Yup. Thanks, Black."

L had watched the house for the past two days and arrived at the conclusion that the information Avant had given him was right. This was a stash house. He'd seen men go in and out of the house for the past two days. Driving all kinds of fancy cars. Jags. Benzes. He'd even seen a Lambo and he thought that was dumb. Like, what the fuck did they think? That the neighbors didn't know what they were up to. Avant had given him all kinds of information about D boys all over the city and so far he'd made a few hundred thousand dollars. But this one might be the biggest lick of them all. He could just tell that these dudes were living the life. One of them was named Bird and that's all he knew.

He knew that because he'd seen the Lambo at a corner store and he'd asked one of the guys for directions. The guy that he'd asked didn't know, so he asked Bird. Avant had mentioned that one of them's name was Bird and Bird was the one that had given the directions. Bird was a tall skinny man with a gooseneck and big feet. He wore an expensive watch. L didn't know the name of the watch, but he'd seen Diddy wearing one of them on Instagram. After he made this robbery, he would post stuff on Instagram and Facebook just like Diddy and all the bitches would like his pics. But most importantly, he'd be set. There was no way that Bird and them were driving Lambos unless they were getting paid.

There wasn't but one way to find out and L intended to do just that. He'd observed that there was no alarm sign in front of the house and that didn't surprise him. If there were drugs there, he knew that they didn't want the police to come to the house for anything. They were probably smoking weed and shit, and if the police came, they would search the house and find drugs. L had heard of a case where a minor had set the alarm off, and the police came to the house and found a garage full of weed. Bird and them didn't seem like they were stupid. They didn't sound like they were from Georgia. Sounded like they may have been from the West Coast and this pissed L off even more. He hated to see out-of-towners coming to Atlanta and make money.

The day after L spoke with them at the gas station, he followed them home and kicked in the door. To his surprise, there were three women and two men downstairs watching TV. L wielded the gun in his hand and ordered everybody to the corner of the room near a closet.

The man L had seen at the gas station said, "What do you want, bruh?"

"I want you to do what the fuck I say. Get your punk ass over in the corner before I blow your fuckin' head off."

One of the girls took hold of the man's arm and said, "Let's do what the man said."

A scruffy looking nigga wearing scuffed up J's and jeans with no shirt and nappy disgusting chest hair said, "Bruh, you don't have to do this. What do you want?"

L fired a shot into his left ass cheek and said, "Where the fuck is Bird?"

The man plopped to the floor and crawled over to the corner.

When they were in the corner, L said, "Where the fuck is the money?" And the work?"

"What work?" Scruffy said.

L aimed the gun at him and said, "I see somebody hasn't learned their motherfuckin' lesson." L slapped the fuck out of him with the gun and said, "Don't you say a motherfuckin' thing else!"

The skinny bitch was crying and pulling her braids. She was about to pull them off her scalp and L said, "What the fuck is wrong with her?"

The other girl said, "Anxiety."

"I'm going to need y'all to calm the fuck down. Calm the fuck down, right now." Then he ordered the girls to have a seat on a sofa that was near the closet.

Scruffy was still crawling and L noticed that he was hiding something under his belly. L fired a shot into the back of his skull. Scruffy died with his eyes wide open and L turned him over on his side and picked up the weapon.

"Ok," L said to the other man. "Get your ass over here."

He made his way toward L and L bound the man's hands with riot handcuffs. Suddenly, L felt cold steel on the back of his neck and before he could aim the gun, the man behind him swatted the gun out of L's hand then fired a shot into L's back. L plummeted to the floor.

The man removed his mask and said, "Who the fuck sent you?"

L was breathing hard as hell. Nervous. His heart was beating fast. His blood pressure had shot up and he was dizzy.

The man placed the gun against L's head and asked again, "Who sent you? Tell me who sent you or I'm going to shoot you in the head."

L said, "Fuck you," and kicked his feet. The man stumbled and L grabbed the man's ankle and bit a hunk of meat out of the man's leg. The man hit him across the head with the gun.

"You bitch-ass nigga. All you can do is bite?" The man laughed as he got up.

L said, "Motherfucker, you might kill me but a year from now, you're going to die too cuz I got full blown AIDS. So shoot me, nigga. Shoot me and put me out of my misery. I don't give a fuck about dying."

The man fired a shot into L's temple. Two days later L's body was found on the side of the road. L's niece updated his Facebook page to "died trying R.I.P. UNK. I will always love you

Chapter 26

DANK HAD BEEN HIDING OUT FOR THE PAST WEEK. LIVING IN A CHEAP hotel on the Southside eating pizza and drinking cold beer while watching Sports Center. He lay on the bed watching the Golden State Warriors against the Hawks. He was sure that the police was looking for him by now. Sure that they had figured out that he'd cut the ankle bracelet. That damn officer that was assigned to watch him while he was on bond visited him every other day religiously. So there was no way they didn't know he was gone. It was official. He was a wanted man. He was just about to doze off when someone knocked at his door. He grabbed his gun. If it was the police, they were going to have to kill him. There was no way that he was going to go out like that. No way was he going to let them pin three bodies on him. No fucking way. He would rather shoot it out with them than to die in prison. "Who is it?"

"It's Nate."

"Who?"

"TeTe sent me."

He opened the door and it was the two men that had visited him in his apartment with TeTe and Todd."'

"What's up?"

"Get your things."

"Where am I going?"

"Chicago."

"Call TeTe." Dank said.

The man phoned TeTe. She answered on the second ring and he passed the phone back to Dank.

"Where am I going?"

"Chicago. Nate has your license and you will be flying under the name Ryan Leaf."

"Wait a minute, that's a football player."

"The white Ryan Leaf is. You're the black Ryan Leaf."

"Okay I guess it will be okay."

"It will be fine. Nate will give you the tickets, a new birth certificate and a driver's license."

"Okay, can you give me some money? I don't have shit."

"Nate is going to give you some money and I'll have a job for you when you get there. Mama has everything already handled for you. I just need you to get the fuck out of here."

"Believe me, I'm ready to go," Dank said. He tossed five T-shirts, four pairs of boxers, three pair of shoes and a digital picture frame of his kids into a suitcase.

"So, how do I get in touch with you when I get where I'm going."

"You'll be staying with my cousin Sherie. She knows how to get in touch with me."

He terminated the call and finished packing.

Nate spotted the beer on the table and said, "Can I have a beer?"

"Yeah, man, go ahead and grab one. Take two, if you want. I don't want any more."

"Cool. I'll take them with us."

Dank was finished packing and they made their way to the car. TeTe was sitting in the car, waiting to drive him to the airport. The flight was leaving at 9:45 p.m. and they had to hurry to make it on time. TeTe was driving as fast as she could when the hood of the car came up. She stopped the car abruptly in the street and asked Dank to hop out and shut the hood. He did and just when she knew the hood was secure, she punched the gas pedal. The car went flying forward bowling his ass over with the car. Then, she backed up and crushed his skull. Then drove away in a hurry.

"What the fuck did you just do?" Nate said.

"What you think did?"

"I thought you were going to send him to Chicago?"

"I was going to send him. I didn't even know I was going to do this. It just happened."

"It just happened?"

"Yeah, something tells me he would have done something stupid and got caught and snitched. I can tell these things."

"You just crushed that man's skull."

TeTe smiled and said, "I know I did. Wasn't it beautiful? Look, he was stupid. I have no room for stupid people and you know what else I have no room for. People that are sympathetic to idiots."

She turned the volume up on the radio. In love With the Coco by O.T Genasis was playing.

•   •   •

Shamari had just finished doing a second set of pushups. He was doing the second with his feet positioned on the edge of his bed. His goal was to be in the best shape of his life. If he had to be in prison, he would at least look and feel good about himself. His roommate, Darren Williams, came into the cell and interrupted him. Darren was a burly man with skin the color of cashew nuts. His face was covered in grey whiskers. He worked in the kitchen, so he usually wore kitchen whites most of the day and today was no exception. Most people called him New Orleans, since he was from Fourth Ward in New Orleans.

"They just called you to the lieutenant's office." New Orleans said.

"Lieutenant's office?" Shamari stood and reached for his T-shirt that was folded neatly on the bed. He slipped into his T-shirt, still breathing hard. Then he stared into the tin mirror on the cell wall. His muscles were bulging and veiny.

New Orleans said, "Muscle man, you need to go on to see what the fuck they're talking about. You know I got all this stolen shit from the kitchen in here and I can't afford for them to shake this cell down. You know if I get caught stealing again, they're going to send me to California somewhere or somewhere farther away. My folks have a hard enough time coming from New Orleans."

"I'm going, man. Lemme get dressed."

New Orleans peeled an orange that he'd stolen from the kitchen. "Don't look like you're getting dressed to me. Looks like you're staring in the mirror. You're going to the LT's office, not the visitation room, pretty boy."

Shamari ignored New Orleans. He was always calling him pretty boy because he took pride in the way he looked and he wanted to stay in shape. Unlike New Orleans, who rarely exercised and ate everything in sight. Shamari grabbed his khaki uniform shirt draped over the edge of the bed. He slid into it, buttoned it all the way up to the top, brushed his hair and headed to the LT's office.

The LT's office was a small office that sat next to the gym. When he entered the office, the lieutenant and the captain were talking. The LT asked Shamari to identify himself and after Shamari had given him his name and inmate number then presented him with his prison ID, the LT told Shamari to follow the captain. The captain led Shamari to the hospital.

"Why am I going to the hospital? There is nothing wrong with me."

"Hey, I just do what I'm told."

Shamari trailed the captain to the hospital and when they arrived, Shamari was escorted inside the doctor's office where he was surprised to see Federal Agents Scott Chandler and David Carroll.

They offered a handshake and after Shamari shook their hands, Agent Chandler said, "You wanted to give us some information about Tyrann Massey a.k.a. Black?"

KINGPIN WIFEYS II, Part 4: Black Widow

Chapter 1

AGENTS CARROLL AND CHANDLER WANTED TO TALK TO SHAMARI before he was sentenced, but he'd told his attorney that he didn't want to talk to them. They wanted to see what he knew and if he was willing to share that information with them. If he helped them, they would help him but Shamari had been adamant that he didn't want to see them. He was determined to take his time like a man, but now that he thought Black was fucking his woman, things were different.

Chandler, the tall blond with movie star good looks, had a friendly demeanor. Carroll was a very matter-of-fact person with dark hair and a serious stern face. Shamari rested his elbows on the table as they stared at him and he at them.

Finally, Chandler said, "So, Tyrann Massey?"

"What do you want to know?"

Chandler said, "So, why now?"

"Huh?"

"Why do you wanna help now?"

Shamari cracked his knuckles and felt guilty about what he was about to do. He was taught never to talk to the police and here he was about to go against everything the OGs taught him. And all because of a woman.

"Why now? I mean, there has to be a reason that you want to give up information," Chandler continued.

"You want your time cut?" Carroll asked.

"I can care less about a motherfuckin' time cut."

"We thought Tyrann was your friend."

"That's what I thought."

"Let me guess. He's sleeping with your woman," the movie star said then laughed loudly.

Silence.

"So you want to get back at him?"

"Maybe."

"Look, we don't really care why you're cooperating. We just wanted to know if you were trying to get a time cut. If we were going to have to ask the judge to reduce your sentence."

"Can he reduce a life sentence?"

"I've seen a guy go from life to ten."

"Really?" Shamari said. Ten years was still a long time, but it didn't seem too bad when you compared it to a life sentence.

"Really. The guy gave up members of the cartel. He got out and we put him in witness protection. He left the program after two years and they found him in Seattle—his body dismembered."

Scott Chandler looked at Carroll as if he wanted him to shut the fuck up. Shamari thought about his Cali connect. They were connected to the Mexican cartel, but there was no way he was going to give them up. They would kill his whole goddamned family.

"No. I just want to keep this about Tyrann."

"What do you got for us?" The movie star kept flicking his ballpoint and it was getting on Shamari's goddamned nerves. It made him feel even more uneasy about what he was about to do. Shamari thought about his reputation in the streets. What his people closest to him would say and most importantly what he was taught.

He said, "I can't."

Carroll said, "What do you mean you can't? You mean to tell me you got us all the way down here and you have nothing to give us!"

"What I was taught is more important than some time cut."

"So you're going to let Tyrann keep fucking your woman?"

"If that's what he want to do."

"Kyrie set you up and Tyrann knew it."

"I can't do it," Shamari said and he dropped his head. He was embarrassed that he'd even thought about giving Black up.

Chandler stood and said, "You'll rot in prison."

Shamari smiled and said, "That's what I planned to do anyway."

He stood and walked through the double doors that led back to the prison yard. A correctional officer named Hankerson was there to escort him back to the dorm. Hankerson was a tall, skinny black man with a pencil-thin goatee. Shamari was familiar with Hankerson since he had been in charge of Shamari's unit.

Hankerson smiled and said, "Damn! They were pissed off at you, bruh."

"You heard them?"

"Yeah."

"I couldn't do it."

Hankerson said, "You're a better man than me. I would have told everything I knew. I guess that's why I'm not a criminal."

"Well, at least you know what you can and cannot do. I respect you for that."

"And I respect you, Brooks. You're always respectable and never give us any problems. You don't deserve to be in here."

Shamari stared at Hankerson and said, "Now I don't want to be in here, but I absolutely deserve to be in here. I did wrong and I have to pay but not for the rest of my life."

Hankerson led Shamari to his dorm. It was almost count time.

Chapter 2

Q AND FRESH ARRIVED IN HOUSTON AND DROVE TO RICO'S DAUGHTER Ivy's house on the Southside side of town. They banged on the door and Ivy opened it up. Ivy was a tall woman with glowing brown skin the color of caramel ice cream and an oval face. She wore tight black spandex shorts and a low-cut t-shirt. Fresh notice it right away and decided that he would fuck her if given the opportunity, even though he was a few years older than she was. She invited them in and led them to a sectional in the tiny apartment.

She said, "Sweet tea or ice water?"

They both declined. Fresh's eyes were on her camel-toe and he began wondering why he hadn't tried to fuck this fine young bitch before. Maybe he would holler at her after Rico's memorial was done.

Ivy noticed that Q wasn't smiling and she said, "You have something bad to tell me, don't you? I don't know why, but I can just feel it."

Q avoided looking in her direction then a single tear rolled down her cheek.

"What happened to my daddy?"

"Your daddy is dead. Murdered by the cartel."

"What? Please tell me you're lying." She covered her face. Her lavender colored nails gripped the top of her forehead. "You're lying. My daddy is not dead. I don't believe you. Why are you lying to me, Q?"

Q made his way over to her side and wrapped his arms around her. He held her then kissed her forehead. "I wish I was lying. I really wish I was."

"Why would you play with me like this?"

Q massaged her back and continued to hold her.

"He's not dead. He's not dead," Ivy continued to cry out.

Q held her, not really knowing what else to do. She cried for the next twenty minutes in denial. Fresh passed her a box of tissue that had been sitting on one of the end tables.

She finally looked up from her hands and said, "How did it happen?"

"All we know is that he was taken down to Mexico and he was murdered down there."

"Who told you this?"

"A good friend of mine."

"A friend of yours murdered my daddy?"

"You know that I wouldn't allow that to happen."

"But you let him get killed."

"I'm sorry." Q avoided her eyes. He knew she was in pain and he couldn't find the right words to ease that pain.

She broke free from his grip. "How did he get killed? Where did he get killed? What part of Mexico? Where is his body? I'm going to the police."

"His body's in Mexico." The truth was that Q didn't know where his body was. He'd called his friend from North Carolina and had him take the head and bury it somewhere in the mountains out there.

"It's in Mexico?"

"Yeah, Mexico." He paused. "If I were you, I wouldn't go to the police."

She said, "So what are you going to do about it? I know my daddy worked for you. What are you going to do about it? You have to get the person who did this to him."

Q avoided her eyes and said, "I'm sorry. I'm sorry it happened."

Ivy made contact with Q and said, "It's not your fault." She hugged Q.

"It is my fault and I promise I'm going to get the people responsible for this," Q said.

She believed him.

Chapter 3

BLACK'S PHONE RANG AN UNFAMILIAR NUMBER. AT THE LAST MINUTE he decided to answer.

"Is this Black?"

"Who the fuck is this?"

"Tara."

"I don't know no Tara."

"Larry's baby mama?"

"L?"

"Yeah, I guess you would call him L."

"What can I do for you?"

"Well, I was calling to let you know that Larry got murdered last night."

"What? Please tell me you're lying."

"I wish I was but he's dead. The police called me and had me come identify the body."

"Do you know what happened?"

"Actually I don't know the details but it was a home invasion that went bad. He was always up to some bullshit. You know he put something on his Facebook page about how he was going to get rich or die trying. I guess his ass died trying."

Black didn't know what to say. He was speechless. He was numb. He couldn't believe that L was gone. He didn't know why he didn't believe it. He's seen a lot of shit in his day, but he just couldn't bring himself to believe L was gone. He didn't want to believe it. Though he and L had their problems, he loved the guy.

"The police took his property and I asked them to give me his phone but they wouldn't. They said it was part of the investigation. Just thought I would let you know, since you were his partner."

"Thank you."

"It's tragic."

"I mean, I don't know what to say. Do you need anything?"

"Like money?"

"Yeah, money."

"No. Larry has given me more money that I can use. Me and Latrell, we're good."

"Latrell?"

"Our daughter."

"I'm glad. I'm sorry this happened."

"Well, if you know Larry like I knew Larry, you know it was bound to happen."

"Yeah."

"Black, can I ask you a question?"

"Yeah."

"Did you know if Larry slept with men?"

There was a long pause. Black contemplated the question and wrestled with his conscience. He had grown to love L like a brother and he didn't want to rat him out but this woman deserved to know. Her life was in danger.

"You don't have to say anything. I think I know."

"Yes, Tara, he slept with men."

"Did he sleep with you?"

"Hell no. People can say a lot of shit about me and a lot of people say a lotta bad shit about me but one thing about me they can't say is that I'm a sword fighter."

"A what?"

"Never mind. I don't fuck with men."

"You know I don't think it's anything wrong as long as you're being honest. But Larry lied to me. He's put me at risk."

"So, if he had told you the truth, you would have still fucked him?"

"No. But what I'm saying is, if you like men say it. At least let me know what I'm dealing with. It's funny because he loved women too. When I was fucking him, he would want to have sex three or four times a night. But that don't mean shit. I swear to you, the state of the black man is tragic. Where are the real motherfuckers?"

"I can feel you on that one."

"Larry told me to have him cremated."

"You're awfully calm for someone who found out that their man sleeps with men."

"I've known for a while, but I just needed confirmation. After I got tested and was told I was okay, there was no reason for me to worry. Me and Latrell will keep getting tested but the doctor was almost certain that we will be fine."

"Good for you."

"But like I was saying, I'm going to cremate him. He has a niece that he loved but other than that, nobody else in his family gave a damn about him."

"Sad."

"He loved you, Black. He looked up to you and he wanted you to like him. He cared about what you thought of him."

"What are you trying to say?"

"Not saying anything. Just letting you know what he thought of you and if you have time, come to the memorial."

"When is it?"

"I don't know yet."

"Let me know and let me know if you need anything."

"Thanks, Black. Take care of yourself. Don't end up like Larry."

"I'll try not to."

"Okay, that's all that I ask."

"You have a good day, Tara. And if you need anything, call me. I'll try to make it to the memorial," Black lied. He knew that there was no way that he was going to make it to the memorial, but it was the right thing to say.

Chapter 4

SHAMARI CALLED BLACK. HE PRESSED 5 TO SKIP THE PRISON recording. Seconds later he was on the line.

"Hey."

"What's up, Mari?"

"Come see me."

"You know I have a record and I can't."

"Take this number down."

"What's the number?"

404-567-9808."

"Who is this?"

"His name is Scooter. Go see him."

"Cool."

"Later."

Black ended the call then he called Scooter.

"Hello?"

"Scooter. This—"

"I know who you are. Mari told you to call me, right?"

"Yeah."

"Where are you?"

"Right now, I'm in Riverdale."

"Come to College Park then call me."

"Okay. Any particular place?"

"Wal-Mart parking lot on Old National. I'll be in a blue Crown Victoria."

Black arrived at the Wal-Mart parking lot and spotted the Crown Victoria with jacked-up tires and Fruit Loop decals on the side. Black thought Scooter was one country-ass dude. He'd thought he'd seen the last of the cars with decals. They had been popular a few years ago, but he hadn't really seen it in a while. Scooter was a skinny-ass dude with braids on each side of his head and a part in the center. He was grinning, showing off his gold buckteeth. A kid about three was in the backseat strapped down in a car seat.

He lowered his window and said, "Black?"

"Yeah."

"Kinda figured that."

"Why? Because I'm black as hell?"

"Pretty much," Scooter said and they both laughed.

"I'm Scooter. Follow me, sir."

"Lead the way."

Scooter led Black into a neighborhood about five minutes away. Lower middle class. The homes were small but the neighborhood was well kept for the most part. Scooter grabbed his little one from the back seat. A boy. Braids down the side of his head and a thick-ass part just like Scooter. The kid had a pacifier in his mouth and Black thought he was too damn big for that but hell, who was he to tell someone how to raise their kids. Black followed Scooter up the stairs and into the house. When they entered the house, there were three more kids around four, five and six years old. They all had Scooter's hairstyle and there was a light-brown woman with an afro puff about to fry some chicken.

She peeked over the counter into the living room and said, "Baby, did you bring me the coconut oil back?"

"Damn! I forgot, baby."

"You know I can't fry the chicken without coconut oil."

"There is sunflower oil at the top of the cabinet."

"I'm not clogging my arteries or the kids arteries up with that junk."

Black just stood at the door and his eyes darted back and forth between Scooter and his girlfriend. Toys were all over the goddamned floor and African art hung on the wall. There was the smell of incense burning. Black noticed two things. Scooter was a hood nigga and a baby-making machine like himself. And Scooter's girlfriend was one of those Afrocentric chicks that irritated the fuck out of Black. He hated all that Black Power shit. He was very surprised that she was even thinking about frying chicken. He would have thought a girl like her would have been vegan.

She turned the burner off and entered the living room where he and Scooter stood. She smiled pleasantly and Black had a chance to take a closer look at her. She was a very attractive woman with a small waist, nice hips and nice tits. Black thought to himself that he would absolutely fuck her though he was almost a hundred percent certain that she had a seventies bush on her vagina. He'd dealt with her kind before.

Afro Puffs had a big grin on her face as she extended her hands and said, "Hey, King! I'm Camille."

Scooter introduced them. "This is Black, baby. Black is one of Shamari's friends."

Black grinned, not because she had just called him King but because his assessment of this bitch was accurate.

"Nice to meet you."

"King, would you mind removing your shoes?"

Black stared at the bitch like she was crazy. The floor was blanketed with popcorn, cheese puffs, broken pencils, crayons, coloring book and Uno cards—and she wanted him to take his shoes off in this mess? Since he had decided that he didn't need the crutches any longer, he obliged and asked, "Why am I here?"

"Bruh, we can go into my office and talk," Scooter said.

Black kicked off his shoes and Camille gathered them and lined them up underneath a coat rack on the other side of the room where the kids were playing.

Inside Scooter's office, Scooter sat behind his desk and Black took a seat on a folding chair across from the chair.

Scooter pointed to the door and said, "Lock that door. Don't want those kids running in here."

Black pushed the door shut and latched it.

"Preciate it, bruh."

Black sat down and Scooter said, "Shamari told me to get you some new paperwork."

"Paperwork?"

"Get you a new license with a new ID so you can go visit him."

"What do you need from me?"

"Nothing. I just need to take a picture of you and you can come back in the morning to pick it up."

Scooter picked up a Cannon DSLR camera from his desk and asked Black to smile. He snapped a picture and Scooter asked, "Is there a name that you would like to use?"

"Cameron Michaels."

Scooter said, "Damn! That was fast. People usually have to think about it."

"The camera gave me the idea for Cameron and Michael is one of my brother's names."

Scooter laughed and said, "Hey, I'm sorry my girl told you to take your shoes off. I saw how you were looking. I know she can be a bit much."

"No problem. It's your house. Your rules."

"The license will be a thousand dollars."

"A thousand dollars for an ID?"

"This ID is going to be one hundred percent official. You can travel with this license. It's a real license, not a fake ID. Just a fake name."

Black dug into his pocket and removed a wad of cash.
"Just bring it with you tomorrow."
"Okay."

Chapter 5

STARR HAD JUST FINISHED GIVING Q THE MOST AMAZING HEAD AND was resting her head on Q's chiseled abs. He was about to doze, but then she said, "Bae, I've been thinking about what you said."

"Huh?" he opened his eyes and caressed her hair.

She made her way up to the head of the bed. They stared at each other and at that moment she was very happy. He kissed her and she liked the fact that he would kiss her even though he knew she had just finished giving him head. Trey would be mad when she wanted a kiss after she finished performing orally. Trey always thought it was like sucking his own dick.

"What did I say?"

"How you wanted to see T.J. That you were his godfather."

"Did I lie?"

She laughed. "No, babe." Then she reached for his manhood again but he denied her.

"Don't tell me you changed your mind and don't want me to see him," Q said.

"No. I want you to see him. I want you to meet my whole family. My mama, my daddy and my sister, Meeka, and her two boys."

"What?"

"Yeah. Although I don't like what you're doing, I do love you. And I want you to be a part of my life. I don't want you to hurt me though, I really don't."

"I'm a man."

"I have low expectations for men. Even my daddy, who I love, ran around on my mama and has a baby outside of the relationship."

"I'm not your daddy."

"But you do have lots of baby mamas. Which tells me that you love the ladies."

"I love this lady." He kissed her on the forehead, and at that moment, she felt wanted by him.

She smiled then stood up from the bed and eased toward the bathroom. He watched her from behind. A white thong crept up the crack of her ass and was just beautiful to him.

His dick came alive and he said, "Where are you going?" He stroked his manhood.

"Can a girl brush her teeth and gargle some mouthwash? I hate having dick breath."

He laughed and he stood and walked to the bathroom. They brushed their teeth together in the Jack and Jill vanities. He dropped his boxers, stepped into the shower and she trailed him. The lukewarm water exploded from the luxury showerhead. She stepped out of the shower and he looked confused.

She said, "I'll be back. I have to get my shower cap." She quickly returned with the cap.

"I can't believe you just did that," Q said.

"I just got my hair done. I don't want to mess it up. Unless you're going to pay for it."

"Trey told me you owned a salon once."

"Yeah, but my cousin runs it. My heart isn't in hair. Every girl in Atlanta that's not stripping or trying to be a reality TV star has a salon. Everybody wants to be an Instagram celebrity."

"I looked at your Instagram page. You have over two hundred followers and it's private."

"Creep," she laughed. "You're a fuckin' stalker."

"Hey, I was just checking you out, but I couldn't see a damn thing."

"I don't want a lot of followers. I just want to do me. I'm not a bragger. I don't need the whole world to see if you buy me something nice."

"Jada has thousands of followers."

"Hey, that's Jada's personality and that's okay but that's not me."

Q said, "Damn, I love you, girl."

She smiled and said, "I'm glad. Can you wash my back, please?"

He lathered her back up with a bar of Dove.

"You don't use body wash?"

"No, I like bar soap."

"Interesting."

"Why?"

She turned and faced him. The water was coming down on her shower cap and attacking his chest.

"Don't take this the wrong way, babe, but you're kind of a metrosexual."

"What?" He laughed and said, "Get the fuck out of here."

"I'm just saying most females use body wash and most metrosexuals do too."

"I don't have body wash."

"And that's surprising."

"I'm a metrosexual because I take pride in how I look?"

"I didn't say that."

"Well, let me say this. I made my first million at twenty-four, so it changed me. It changed the way I thought and the way I dressed."

"So it's time to get out the business."

"It's gonna happen."

She faced the water and he lathered her back then he palmed her ass cheeks and she whimpered.

"No," she said.

He ignored her and continued to massage her ass, each touch becoming more and more sensual.

"Please stop," she said.

He kissed her neck and she wanted to resist but she couldn't. She turned and locked lips with him. He hoisted her body up against the glass shower cage.

"You're going to break it."

"I'll replace it."

He sat her down and she bent over and he inserted his penis deep inside. The water cascaded onto her soapy back as he thrust, his thighs smacking hard against her ass. The shower cap toppled and he pulled her hair while he fucked her doggy style. She loved it. Then she realized that when she resisted earlier, she was just pretending. She wanted Q. The man she loved. The businessman. The plug. The thug. A boss. He kept slapping her ass hard, her head occasionally tapping the glass. There was nowhere for her to run and nothing to hold on to. She had to take that punishment. She enjoyed his dick and she could not wait to welcome him to the family.

Chapter 6

BLACK RECEIVED THE DRIVER'S LICENSE FROM SCOOTER AND AS promised it was an official state document. Black held up it up next to his real license and the only difference was the name. Twenty minutes after he picked up the license, Shamari called and after a few rings Black bypassed the prison recording and pressed five. Shamari's voice was on the other end.

"Hey, can I speak to Cameron Michaels?"

Black was laughing his ass off. "I just got one question," Black said.

"What?"

"How in the hell do you know Scooter and his girl?"

"Man, they grew up in the hood. Them two have been together for years. They look like an odd pair, don't they?"

"In a million years I wouldn't have thought that a hood nigga like that would be with some Erykah Badu chick."

"Man, Camille is from the hood, just like us. Her brother did time for drugs. Don't let that act fool you, bruh. She started hanging in Little Five Points about ten years ago. Met some five percenters then she started that Black Power shit. She's cool though, bruh! They are good people. Just some people from the hood trying to raise their kids."

"I got ya. I trust you one hundred percent. I know you wouldn't put me in a fucked-up position. That never once crossed my mind. I trust you. We're like brothers."

"Come see me tomorrow. I've spoken with my counselor and asked him if he could give me a special visit and he said he would. So you're on my list for a special visit, but you're going to have to come within forty-eight hours."

"Look out for me tomorrow at two thirty."

"Okay."

The next day Black entered the prison visiting room. As soon as he sat down, a guy that he had known since juvenile detention spotted him. Tookie was a short guy with a big-ass forehead. He was serving a life sentence for operating a major drug ring.

Tookie said, "Black."

Black just grinned at him and threw up his hand. He knew that he wasn't supposed to converse with inmates and plus he didn't want his cover blown. He was lucky that most people didn't know his real name was Tyrann so not many could dispute that Cameron Michaels was not his real name.

Tookie knew his name but clearly a guy that had a life sentence was the least of Black's worries. Tookie gave Black a signal that he wanted his phone number. Black shook his head indicating that he would send his number, but there was no chance in hell he was going to send Tookie his number. He didn't want to be become friendly with someone that he hadn't seen since he was eighteen, and besides, what could they do for each other. Seconds later, Shamari appeared.

Black stood up and embraced Shamari. "Damn. You been working out hard."

Shamari's chest was extra pronounced and his biceps were swollen. He turned up the sleeves of his shirt and kissed his arms before sitting down across from Black.

"Seriously, man. You're looking good," Black said.

"I try to take care of myself."

Tookie was three tables over waving, trying to get Black's attention.

Shamari said, "You know Tookie?"

"Yeah we were locked up together as juveniles."

Black indicated to Tookie that he would give Shamari the number.

"You want him to have your number?"

"Hell no! I'll send him my Nana's number."

Shamari laughed and then he said, "I should have known that there would be somebody in here that knows your black ass."

"Actually, it's quite a few dudes here that know me."

"I know. I met a few. What I mean is in the visiting room."

"What's been up?"

"I need money, bruh."

"What? You got money that you can't even spend."

"Look, man. I don't know what's going on with Jada but I can't depend on her to be there for me. So I want to make some money and I want you to keep it for me or you can give it to my sister Tangie. You know my sister, right?"

"I've seen her but I don't know her."

"Okay. I'll put you two in touch."

"I don't have a connect. I thought I did. Actually, I thought I had Trey's connect but they ain't going out for dealing with a nigga like me so I'm back to square one." "What do you mean they don't want to deal with you?"

"You know I like to get violent if necessary. A lot of people can't handle that."

"You have my connect. I told Jada to give you the number. So you can call them. Did you call them?"

"No. I didn't have time."

"I can call my people out in Cali and you can go out there and see them." Shamari paused then he said, "I forgot. You're afraid to travel and get the work."

"I have a way to get it back." Black would get Sasha to lease him a plane.

Shamari scanned the room trying to make sure nobody heard him. Nosey-ass Tookie was still staring in their direction. "You still got the number, right?"

"I might have it somewhere. I will have to look for it."

Shamari said, "Give me four dollars. I'm going to the vending machine and when I come back I'm going to give you your change along with a piece of paper with the connect's name and number."

Black passed him the four one-dollar bills.

Shamari dashed to the vending machine and returned with two packs of cheese crackers and a Coke. He passed Black the paper with the connect's number on it.

"I'll give them a call tomorrow."

"I spoke with him and he's waiting on you."

"He's Mexican?"

"Yeah, the black dude is in jail for some bullshit. He will be out soon, but right now, you have to deal with the Mexican. But it will be better for you."

Shamari opened the cheese crackers and offered Black one. Black took one and said, "Damn, you should have bought me a soda."

Shamari pushed the Coke over to the side of the table and said, "Take this."

"You sure?"

"I'm positive. I hardly ever drink sodas. The only reason I got this was because I needed a reason to pass you the note."

"Okay, I see you're on your Richard Simmons shit."

"Who the hell is that?"

"The gay, white dude that be jumping around in tight ass shorts working out."

"Oh fuck, no." Shamari said, before becoming serious. "How is Jada?"

"I haven't seen Jada." Black popped the top of the soda and then said,

"You know what? I was really pissed that you thought I was fucking with Jada."

"Look, I'm sorry. You know how your mind races in here. You know how it can be?"

"But I'm your brother. Do you really think I am that dirty? Do you think I will fuck anyone?"

Shamari looked away. He didn't respond to Black.

Black gulped down some Coke. There was silence at the table before Black said, "I can't believe you thought that."

"She told me she had somebody."

"She didn't say that somebody was me, did she?"

"No."

"It's not me, bruh."

"Who is it?"

Black and Shamari locked eyes and Black really wanted to tell Shamari who Jada was fucking. Shamari was his friend but since Jada didn't want to tell him, he wouldn't. "I don't know."

"Okay. Let's change the subject."

"No, let's not change the subject. I need you to tell me that you believe me."

"I believe you, bruh. Let's get this money."

Chapter 7

JADA WENT TO THE GYM AND GOT IN A GOOD HOUR AND A HALF workout. When she drove up to her house, she checked her mailbox. There were several utility bills and a postcard from Shamari that read: I have accepted the fact that I'm going to spend the rest of my life in here, not because of something you did, but because of the choices I made. Just want to let you know that neither space nor time can change the love that I have for you. Love, Shamari

She wanted to cry and she was just about to close the mailbox when she spotted a pink piece of paper. She figured it was a solicitation for a local restaurant, perhaps a pizza delivery service, but she noticed that the script was written with a magic marker. Bitch, your days are numbered.

Jada's hand trembled. She was terrified. Who the fuck had written this note? Who was that brazen to come to her house? Whoever it was, they were some bold motherfuckers. Was it the same people that murdered Big Papa? Was it the men that tried to assassinate her? Maybe these people were the same people. Maybe they were inside her home. But then she realized that they couldn't be inside her home because the alarm had been set. She went inside, disarmed the alarm then reset it. Then she called Black.

"Hello?"

"Get over here right away," Jada said.

"What's wrong with you?"

"Just come over here."

"I went to see Shamari today and he's swearing that I'm fucking you."

"Look, I don't give a damn about what Shamari thinks. Can you come over right away?"

"Yes. Give me twenty minutes."

"Okay." Jada ended the call then went to the fridge to get a mini bottle of Barefoot Moscato. She needed a drink. After staring at the Moscato for a few moments, she decided that she needed something much stronger than wine. She needed vodka. She made her way to the cabinet and retrieved some Patron. She poured herself a glass of Patron to calm her fucking nerves. After three shots of Patron, the doorbell sounded. She peeked outside and saw a pickup truck in her driveway that she'd never seen before. Her phone rang. It was Black.

"Hello?" Jada said.

"I'm outside."

"That's you in the pickup truck?"

"Yeah. It's my old man's."

She opened the door. She was standing there with tight spandex workout pants on and Black was finding it very hard not to look at her camel toe. Her ass looked sensational but there was no way that he would go there with her. Especially now, since Shamari thought they were fucking around. She latched the door and she made her way into the kitchen. He followed and they sat down at her kitchen table. She offered him a drink and he declined. She poured herself another glass and downed it.

"What is going on?" Black asked.

She passed him the note.

"Where did you get this?"

"It was in my mailbox."

"So you don't know where it came from?"

"Look, I told you that somebody tried to kill me a few weeks ago and then my friend Big Papa ended up dead."

"Who the fuck is Big Papa?"

"Big Papa was my friend. He was Shakur's friend as well."

"And so you think that the person that killed Big Papa left the note?"

"Yes. Because they know that I know you. There are people that think I'm the reason Shakur got murdered."

"Who?"

"Detroit niggas. That's all I know. I don't know who they are but somebody is going to try to kill me and I gotta get the fuck out of here. I gotta find somewhere to go."

Black was staring at her nice-ass tits spilling out of the Nike sports bra. Though they were fake they looked nice to him at this moment. He could see why Shamari was worried, but he knew that there was no way that Jada would ever fuck him even if he was the kind of guy that would sleep with his friend's girl. She just didn't give him the energy.

"Black, my face is up here." Jada put her two fingers in front of her eyes. She caught him peeking and he was embarrassed.

"Can you change shirts? It's distracting," Black said.

"What the fuck?" She protested before disappearing into the back and returned wearing a long t-shirt.

He smiled and said, "Now, can I have a drink? This is a lot to think about."

She poured him a shot of Patron. He tried not to look at her ass but he couldn't help it.

When she turned around and said, "Look, Black, what's wrong with you? Why are you watching me like that? I changed my shirt and now you're still being disrespectful as hell."

"Look, I'm sorry."

"Get it out your mind."

"Look, regardless of what people think about me, I wouldn't try you."

She poured the liquor and said, "Because you know I would shut it all the way down."

"That and there is Lani and Shamari."

"True. I'm going to need you to focus. I need to get the fuck out of here and I need you to be here when I leave."

"What do you mean?"

"I want you to be here when I pack my shit up."

"You found somewhere to go?"

"No, I'm staying here tonight and then I'm going to get a gun tomorrow."

"That's a good idea." Black downed the liquor and turned then he stared at his watch and said, "I gotta go."

"I don't wanna stay here by myself."

"Call Fresh."

"He's in Houston."

"Where am I gonna sleep?"

"I have a pullout sofa."

"I don't wanna stay here."

"Look, motherfucker, it's your fault that I'm in the middle of this bullshit in the first place."

"I'll stay," Black said.

"I'm gonna shower and you can watch TV until then. When I'm done maybe we can go grab some Chinese food around the corner."

"They don't deliver?"

"Look, I don't want nobody to come here. I don't trust anybody."

After Jada showered, she returned wearing jeans and a t-shirt. With her hair braided, she looked like Pocahontas. They rode together to the Chinese restaurant in Black's dad's truck and after they returned they sat and talked over beef and broccoli and shrimp. After they were done, she changed into a pair of silk pajamas. She brought Black a blanket and pillow and pulled the sofa bed out.

"The thermostat is in the hallway. If you get too hot, you can turn the air on but don't freeze me. I know how guys can be; always wanting the place to be cold."

He smiled and she said, "There is food in the fridge if you get hungry again."

"I'm good unless your mama made some more macaroni?"

"No."

He made a sad face and she laughed. He watched her ass bounce in those silk pajamas. He could see her lace panties underneath. When he was sure she was gone for the night, he removed his clothes, folded them and placed them on an armchair across from the sofa. Then he pulled the covers over his head thinking that no matter how much he loved Shamari, it would be very tempting if Jada called him into the bedroom. He thought about Lani and wondered if she was looking down on him. He removed his penis from his boxers and stroked himself until the cum exploded into the palm of his hand. He dozed finally with a firm grip on his dick.

Chapter 8

BLACK AND JADA ENTERED TETE'S HOME. BUTTERFLY WAS THERE AND she immediately started staring at Jada.

Finally Black said, "Jada, I want you to meet my friend Butterfly."

Butterfly was blushing while she stared at Jada. Dressed in a pink ballerina dress she looked incredible.

Jada kneeled and said, "Oh my God! Butterfly, you're so beautiful."

Butterfly was smiling hard. Then she turned to Black and said, "When are you going to let me meet your daughter?"

"Soon," Black said."

Butterfly made a sad face then said, "You should take us to see the Avengers."

Jada laughed and said, "Yeah, Black, take the kiddies to see the Avengers."

TeTe was at the top of the stairway glancing down and she said, "What do we say to Ms. Jada for calling you beautiful, Butterfly?"

"Thank you, Ms. Jada."

TeTe said, "Was she begging again?"

"No, she wants me to take her and my daughter to see the Avengers."

"I already told her that I was going to take her."

Black said, "How about we all go together. You know I love the kiddies."

Jada said, "You should love them, you made enough of them."

When TeTe reached the bottom of the staircase, she just gave Butterfly the eye.

Butterfly said, "I know you want me to leave."

"Exactly. Now get your little grown ass out of here."

Butterfly disappeared into her bedroom and TeTe led Jada and Black through the living room into a den.

Jada said, "Your home looks amazing."

"Thank you, Jada."

TeTe sat on the sofa and Black sat next to her. Jada sat on a recliner that was next to a sectional.

TeTe said, "Where are my manners?" She turned to Jada. "Have something to drink?"

"No. I'm good."

TeTe faced Black and rubbed his leg. "Anything for you, baby?"

"I'm good too."

"Yes you are." She laughed a wicked laugh and she eyed his package.

"Be good."

"Spank me."

"Not around Jada."

"I can leave."

"Jada has an issue."

TeTe turned to Jada. "You know any problem of yours is a problem of mine, Jada."

"Show her the note."

Jada passed TeTe the note.

TeTe ripped the goddamned note into pieces. "Who the fuck are these bitch-ass niggas"

"Shakur's friends. Brothers. I don't know."

"Where are they?"

"I don't know."

"Look, I'm a big girl I can handle myself," Jada said.

"Nobody is going to ever threaten me and get away with it. Man, woman or child," TeTe said.

"Too many people have died already," Jada said.

"What are you saying, Jada?"

"Don't make a big deal out of it. I'll be fine."

TeTe shrugged her shoulders then turned to Black. "She doesn't need help."

"Just tell her that I'm not the reason that somebody tried to kill her. I didn't kill Shakur."

"I didn't kill him either," TeTe said.

"Just tell her that I didn't have anything to do with it," Black said.

"Wait a minute! Are you bitching up on me? I didn't even know these people. They were after you and not me," TeTe said.

"That's not what I meant, babe," Black said.

"What the fuck did you mean? Seems to me you are trying to blame every goddamned thing on me."

"I just want all the drama to stop," Jada said.

TeTe said, "All the drama has stopped as far as I'm concerned."

"What about the people that left the note?" Black asked.

"Jada said she'll be fine, so it's not our business," TeTe said.

"No, I can take care of myself." Jada stood then Black stood and finally TeTe rose and said, "Now I'm confused as hell about this meeting."

Jada said, "I just want peace."

"Sometimes you need conflict to get your point across."

After the conversation, there was no doubt in Jada's mind that TeTe was capable of having someone murdered.

TeTe escorted Jada to the door and said, "If you have any problems, let me know."

"I will. Thanks so much."

Black kissed TeTe and he grabbed a handful of her ass. He whispered, "You don't have on panties."

"Is that a problem?

"Why would that be a problem?"

"Are you coming back?"

"Yes. And you're gonna be coming back to back."

She smiled and said, "That's what I want to hear."

Chapter 9

STARR'S MOM WAS NAMED WANDA. SHE WAS A PLEASANT LADY AND looked like an older version of Starr but with wider hips although her waist was still very tiny. When she was younger, all the hustlers wanted her. Her father had been a preacher and he had forbidden her from dating drug dealers. Then Starr's father, Ace, came along. Ace was a star football player, who peddled a little weed on the side. He had plans of going to college on a football scholarship until he was accused of raping a white girl. He was ultimately found not guilty but the incident had blown his football scholarship. Wanda didn't want to have anything to do with Ace after the incident, because though Ace was found not guilty of rape. It had come out in trial that Ace had in fact been having consensual sex with the young woman. Months later, Wanda finally forgave him. Ace's small-time weed dealing led to cocaine dealing and soon Ace was one of the biggest dealers in Atlanta.

Starr's family sat at the kitchen table. Starr's mother Wanda, Ace, T.J., her sister Meeka and Meeka's sons DeVante and DeMontre. Meeka stood and introduced herself to Q and then Ace and Q exchanged hellos. Ace made Q feel at ease because he wasn't some stuffy-ass old dude and Wanda gave Q a big hug as if she was welcoming him to the family. He certainly felt embraced.

DeVante said, "You must be rich."

Q felt a little embarrassed and said, "No."

"I bet he ain't got more bread than Trey had," DeMontre said. He was the older twin by six minutes.

"That Ferrari cost over two hundred racks." DeVante said.

Q had driven his yellow Ferrari Spider. It stood out in Starr's parent's neighborhood but the neighborhood was a low crime area and he knew it would be okay, but man did it draw a lot of attention. People were staring like hell as they drove past the house.

"Will y'all shut the hell up and quit asking this man a hundred questions?" Ace said.

Starr turned to Q and said, "I'm sorry."

Starr helped her mom prepare everybody a plate. Dinner was a pot roast with carrots and gravy, mashed potatoes, corn and a lemon cake for dessert.

Q said, "This food smells delicious."

"Can't nobody cook better in Georgia than my mama," Meeka said.

"I can believe that."

"That's why I married her," Ace said and slapped her on the ass.

Wanda said, "Would you stop?"

"Nasty old man," DeVante said.

"What? Just cuz you think I'm old don't mean I can't get me none."

Meeka said, "Daddy, that's TMI."

"What the hell is TMI?"

"Too much information,"

"Everybody in this house except for Q is here because of me, I made all of y'all."

"You didn't make me," Wanda said.

"Daddy, chill," Starr said.

"Chill, my ass. If Q is going to be a part of this family, he needs to know how I am."

Q was eating the hell out of his pot roast and he said, "I don't mind at all. Be yourself, sir."

"I don't like nobody calling me sir. I'm in my fifties, not seventies."

Meeka said, "So, Q, I hear you are from Houston. My girlfriend Nicole is from Houston. She said all the guys in Houston is short, but I know that's a lie cuz Slim Thug from Houston. Do you know Slim Thug? Cuz if you do, I'mma need you to set me up with him with his tall fine ass." Then she turned to the twins and said, "That's right. Slim Thug will be your stepdaddy."

Everybody was laughing their asses off and then Wanda said, "Let's say grace."

"My bad. I already started eating." Q was embarrassed.

Ace said, "It's okay, we don't always thank God for the food. Only when we remember."

"Why don't Q say grace," Wanda said.

Q bowed his head and said, "God, thanks for this magnificent food I am about to receive and for this magnificent family but most of all, thanks for the incredible woman that you have saw fit to put my life. Amen."

Ghetto-ass Meeka said, "Damn, girl, you got you a keeper and he's a baller. How did y'all meet?"

Ace said, "Yeah, how did y'all meet?"

Starr said, "I don't want to talk about that right now." The truth was that she was embarrassed that Q was Trey's friend and she didn't want her family all up in her business.

"Oh, I get it. You met him on one of those matchmaking sites. One of those Sugar Daddy sites."

"I ain't met nobody on the Internet."

"Why you so secretive, lil sis? I want me a Q. Hell I'll even take an X or Y or a Z." Meeka laughed.

Starr was getting pissed and said, "Hey, this is not the right time to talk about it."

Ace said to Meeka, "Will you shut the hell up and eat."

Starr was super embarrassed and she was starting to second-guess her decision to bring Q to dinner.

Q said, "I knew Trey before he died. We were friends."

The table was quiet and Starr was wondering why in the fuck did Q have to say that. She felt so embarrassed. She felt like a thot.

One of the twins said, "I miss Uncle Trey."

"Trey was a good guy." Ace said.

Meeka said, "That's all you had to say. It don't matter if you smashing the homie. Hell, Trey gone. He can't do nothing for you."

If it wasn't for her mother, Starr would have dragged Meeka's ass across the table and beat her down.

"I'm not smashing the homie."

Meeka turned to her mama and said, "Ma, can I have a glass of wine?"

"You ain't going to drink all my wine, girl."

"I'm not trying to drink all your wine. I asked for one glass." Then she turned her attention to Starr and said, "If Trey and Q were homies, you are smashing the homie!"

"Whatever."

Wanda said, "Meeka, will you shut the hell up."

"For what? I ain't even do nothing. Y'all always taking Starr's side. Acting like her shit don't stank. Her shit stank just like everybody else."

Starr placed her hands over T.J.'s ears and Meeka said, "He's gonna hear worse shit than that. The world is cold, baby girl." Meeka laughed then stood and poured herself a glass of wine, totally ignoring the fact that her mother had told her that she couldn't have a glass of wine before taking her seat back at the table.

"Why did you even invite them over here in the first place?" Starr asked her mother.

"You invited me, bitch. And I don't need an invitation to come to my mama and daddy's house. This ain't your house. Everything don't belong to you, Starr."

Starr stood up and said, "Say one more word to me, bitch, and I will drag your ass."

Meeka stood and said, "I'm supposed to be scared. " Meeka laughed. "Bitch, I ain't hardly afraid of yo' ass."

Ace said, "Both of y'all sit y'all asses down right now."

Starr grab Q by the arm and said, "Babe, let's go."

Q said, "No, it's okay. Plus I wanna finish up this good food."

Wanda said, "Let Q finish eating his food." Then she apologized to Q.

Q said, "It's okay. There is nothing to apologize for. I wish my family could get together and have a meal. At least y'all are close."

"Your family ain't close?"

"Not at all. One of my brothers drowned when we were little, the other one is in jail and my sister is in Germany. We don't speak too often."

"What about your parents?"

"My dad is dead and my mom is back in Houston. I have a good relationship with her."

"Good. That means you'll take care of my daughter. I want some more grandbabies besides these three knuckleheads." Ace said. He rubbed T.J.'s head and said, "T.J., don't you want a brother or sister?"

"Yes, I want a brother and a sister."

Ace laughed and said, "That means y'all better go to work."

Wanda said, "Q, you have kids?"

Ace said, "You know damn well that black man got kids. It's just a question of how many baby mamas."

"I got three kids."

"How many baby mamas?"

"Two."

"That's not that bad for a black man," Ace laughed.

"Well not as bad as yo' ass." Wanda stared at Ace, reminding him of his indiscretions during their relationship and Ace decided it was time for him to shut the fuck up. He didn't want his wife bringing up old shit.

After they finished their food, Ace told Q to come to the den with him.

"You smoke cigars?"

"I do."

Ace passed him a cigar and said, "Q, I like you. I like you a lot, but I'm going to tell you point blank, nobody puts their hands on my daughter and gets away with it. Understand me?"

"I don't beat women."

"Look, I don't give a damn about other women. I give a damn about my daughter. Understand me?"

"What are you saying?"

"I'm telling you the same thing I told Trey. The day that you touch my daughter is the day that you die. It ain't going to be no 'I'm sorry bullshit' and I don't give second chances."

"I won't need a second chance because I don't fight women."

"Good."

Q laughed at Ace. He respected hm. He knew that he could fuck Ace's old ass up but he chose to be respectful to him. The man loved his daughter and there was nothing wrong with that.

Q puffed his cigar and said, "Is there anything else?"

"Nothing. I have one rule and that's it. What am I going to do? Tell you not to sleep around when that's what I did. Hell, I'm no role model. Hustlers are going to sleep around."

"What makes you think I'm a hustler?"

"It's not what I think. It's what I know and I know you're a hustler. I used to do the same shit."

"I got businesses."

"You may have legitimate businesses, but you're a hustler. Man, don't bullshit me."

"I am, but—"

"You're getting out the game. That's what they all say. I said it too and I did—when the Feds took me away and all my so-called friend ratted on me. Starr and Meeka had to grow up without me and I wound up doing more damage than good because they ended up with men just like me."

"Starr is a good woman."

"She is and I hate to say it but she is my favorite. She's a smart girl who knows how to make money legally. I mean how much money do we have to have anyway? We just had a great meal and I have a great family that I hope becomes your family one day. You don't need a lot."

"What are you trying to say?"

"You'll never make enough money. Don't go to your grave chasing money. Learn from my mistakes."

"I like you, Ace."

"I like you too, young brother."

Ace's cell phone rang and Ace answered before it could ring again. "I told you don't call this damn phone."

He hung up and looked at Q embarrassed. "As you young people say, that was my side bitch."

They both laughed their asses off.

• • •

"I saw a quote one day that said, 'He tasted her and realized that he had been starving.'" Q said.

"Jodi Picoult."

"Who?"

"That's where the quote came from, actually it's 'I tasted her and realized that I had been starving.' It's a lesbian relationship."

"Well, I like it better 'He tasted her and realized he had been starving.' "

"Okay."

He turned to her and they made eye contact. He said, "That's how I feel when I'm with you. I have waited all my life to meet somebody like you and I have been searching my whole life for happiness and I realize that I have finally found it with you."

Starr teared up and said, "That was beautiful, Q."

"No, seriously. I mean if there was anything good that came out of Trey's death, it would have to be this and I don't mean it in a negative way because you know how I feel about Trey."

"I think Trey is happy right now."

"You think so?"

"Trey was no hater. He wanted me to be happy and I know he loved you."

"How is his mother doing? Does she need anything?"

"I took T.J. over the other day. She's fine. She's doing okay. She has plenty of money. She had just gotten back from Miami, so she's living her life."

"Good, but seriously, Starr, you complete me." He leaned into her and kissed her.

"You know I thought about oral sex when you started with that quote, right?"

"You want me to taste you?" He laughed.

"Why not?"

"Maybe tonight."

"I'm going to hold you to it."

Before Q could respond, his phone rang.

"Hello?"

"What you doing?" Fresh asked.

"Lying in the bed with my woman."

"Cupcaking, huh?"

"If that's what you want to call it."

"Just called to let you know I got me a new place."

"Oh yeah. Where is it?"

"It's a townhome in Buckhead but I haven't moved in yet. I'm still at the hotel for a couple of weeks until I get the place furnished. Maybe Starr can help me decorate it."

"Maybe."

"Meet me at Gladys Knight's Chicken and Waffles."

"I'm going to need an hour." He terminated the call.

"Okay, baby, I need you to get a shower. We're going to Gladys Knight's."

"Right now?"

"Yeah."

Starr made a sad face, but she stood up from the bed and seconds later she was in the shower.

When Starr and Q arrived at Gladys Knight's, they found Fresh in the front of the restaurant. When they got closer, Starr realized that Fresh was there with a woman that wasn't Jada. Q and Starr sat across the booth from the happy couple.

"This is Brianna." Brianna was short with a doll face, shoulder length hair and very curvy. She was wearing a pink Maxi dress that was very flattering to her figure.

Starr shook Brianna's hand and said, "Nice to meet you. I'm Starr."

"What a pretty name," Brianna said.

"Thank you."

"This is big brother Q." Fresh said.

"I've heard a lot about you."

Brianna stood and said, "Baby, order me the garlic shrimp. I'm going to the restroom."

Brianna's was wearing black leggings and her ass looked like two soccer balls. Fresh and Q watched her go to the bathroom.

When Starr saw that Q was staring she said, "You see something you like?"

"No I was just—"

"You was just watching Brianna's ass."

"Maybe."

"What do you mean maybe? That's exactly what you were doing."

Fresh was laughing his ass off and Starr said, "You know this is some foul shit you're doing, right?"

"What do you mean?"

"You know how Jada feels about you. And I didn't want to meet this girl. As a matter of fact, Q, I'm leaving."

Fresh said, "What are you talking about?"

"You know damn well what I'm talking about. Jada likes you and you have led her to believe that you like her."

"What?"

"Okay, so you don't be buying Jada gifts and spending time with her?"

"Yeah I do, but I never told her we're in a relationship."

"I'm going to tell you like this. You better make it clear that you ain't in no relationship with her because if Jada see your little girlfriend, she is going to beat the brakes off her ass. I'm telling you."

"Whatever."

Starr nudged Q and said, "Let me out of this booth."

Q stood and Starr slid out of the booth and said to Q, "Are you talking me home or should I call Uber. I can't be a part of this circus."

Fresh said, "Circus?"

"Circus! Because you're a clown-ass nigga."

"You don't know shit about me."

"And I don't want to know shit about you. I know what I know! And what I know about you ain't good."

Starr made her way toward the entrance. Q was trailing her and on the way out, they ran into Brianna.

Starr said, "Nice to meet you, Brianna."

"Why are you leaving?"

"An emergency came up."

The ladies shook hands and seconds later, Starr and Q jumped into his car and drove away.

Starr called Jada and told her to come over right away. Thirty minutes later, Jada rang the doorbell. T.J. opened the door and Jada kneeled and greeted him with a big hug. He was smiling so hard.

"Mom, it's Auntie Jada!" he called out.

Jada was surprised that he had called her auntie, but she loved it. She had a niece that she rarely saw because her sister was in and out of rehab.

Jada said to T.J., "You're getting so big."

"I know. I'm going to be tall like a basketball player when I grow up."

"You like basketball?"

"Not really. I like football and karate. I played flag football last year. Mom said she's going to let me play tackle this year."

"All right big boy. Let me see your muscles."

TJ made a muscle and Jada said. "Wow."

Starr appeared and said, "T.J., go play with your PlayStation. Let me and Auntie Jada talk."

"Okay, I'll take the auntie role," Jada said and they laughed.

When T.J. closed his door, Starr sat on the sofa on opposite ends.

"You're a really good woman and I'm glad to have you as a friend."

Starr smiled and said, "You too. I consider us sisters. I actually introduced Q to the family the other day and I was about to whoop my sister's ass. I mean she showed her ass."

"What happened?"

"She was saying all kinds of foul shit. Talking about I think my shit don't stank and then when she found out that Q and Trey were friends, said I was smashing the homie."

"Oh, that's fucked up."

"My sister has a foul mouth."

"Lani told me your sister was crazy."

"But I don't want to talk about her. How have you been?"

"I'm doing fine. Why do you ask?"

"I heard about your friend Big Papa. I'm sorry to hear about that."

"I'm okay," Jada thought about Big Papa having her set up to get killed but she didn't want to think about him.

"Listen, I gotta tell you something and I don't know how you're going to take it."

"What do you mean, 'you don't know how I'm going to take it'? Is it bad news?"

"Depends on how you take it."

Now Starr was pissing Jada the fuck off. She was trying to be nice, but she wished Starr would get to the fucking point.

"Tell me."

"I saw Fresh with a chick today."

Jada was calm but so much was going through her head. Who was this bitch and what did she have on her? Where were they? Who was this ho to him? But Jada wouldn't ask Starr nothing. She simply said, "Oh really?" She kept a straight face and pretended like that shit didn't bother her in the slightest.

"Yeah, he called Q this morning and had us meet him at Gladys Knight's and he introduced me to her."

"Who is the bitch?" Jada couldn't remain calm any longer.

"I don't know. Some chick named Brianna."

"And he said that she was his girlfriend?"

"No, but he said that you and him wasn't in a relationship and I said you know how she feels about you and this is some bitch-ass shit that you're pulling. I left because I wasn't down with that."

Jada was fuming. She wanted to fuck somebody up. She wanted to fuck Fresh up and though she knew she couldn't whip his ass, she would try her damnedest. She was also embarrassed that Starr had seen him with someone else but she was thankful that she had brought that to her attention.

"If it makes you feel any better, she didn't have anything on you. Seemed a little country and kind of naive which is why I didn't call you. I know that it would have been bad if you would have saw her."

"Well, it would have been bad on his ass. Not her because you're right, he was leading me to believe that it was a possibility. He was right, though. We are not in a relationship but he had me thinking that there was a possibility of one."

Starr scooted closer to Jada and gave her a big hug and said, "It's going to be all right, baby girl."

Chapter 10

JADA BANGED ON FRESH'S HOTEL SUITE. HE OPENED THE DOOR shirtless wearing blue boxers. It was obvious that he'd been sleeping.

He said, "Why are you beating on my door so damn hard and how did you know I was here? How did you get up here?" Fresh wondered how in the hell was she able to get on the elevator without a key.

Jada ignored his silly-ass questions. "Can I come in or is that bitch in there?" She stood there with her hands on her hips.

He stepped aside and she marched right on in. They sat down in the living room area of the suite.

"Why did you just pop up over here? How would you like it if I popped up over your house?"

"Uh oh. There is the bullshit. You're just like all these other motherfuckas."

He stood and walked over to the kitchen counter and poured himself a glass of Hennessy. "I see right now I'm going to have to calm my nerves."

"You do that if you need to."

Fresh stared at her. He was confused as hell. "What is all the hostility about?"

"You know damn well what it's about."

"Oh, okay I get it. You tripping because of what your girl told you about Brianna."

"Look, I ain't hardly tripping. You ain't seen tripping. I can show you tripping. Do I look like I'm tripping?"

He sipped his liquor and laughed and his laughing was pissing her the fuck off.

"What's so goddamned funny, Fresh?"

"You're funny. This shit ain't that serious to me."

"Fuck you!"

"First of all, why are you mad? What did I do to you? I ain't never say we were in a relationship."

The room was silent as Fresh walked over and poured himself another drink. Jada watched him, thinking that he was so goddamned fine and how stupid she was for thinking a man like that would want something serious. He was too much of a pretty boy and too much of a player. She thought about Big Papa and how she had done him. How she had done Shamari and Craig. Was this karma? She had finally met her match and this shit wasn't fair. It wasn't fair that she had grown to have feelings for him. Feelings that he obviously didn't reciprocate. She wanted to cry but she would not let him see her breaking down.

"Did I ever tell you that we were together? Did I ever tell you that I wasn't going to see somebody else?"

She stood and said, "No, you're right."

She turned and was walking toward the door when he jumped in front on her.

"Will you please move?"

"No. You came over here to talk. Let's talk."

"There is nothing to talk about. You're right. You never told me that we were in a relationship."

"Have a seat."

She sat down and he said, "Help me understand why you felt the way you felt."

"Look, you didn't have to say that we were in a relationship, but let me tell you that when you are spending time with a female, you're sending her the message that she is special."

"Jada, you are special to me."

She laughed and said, "I guess the next bitch is special too."

"Jada, I'm sorry I can't give you what you want."

"Don't be sorry. I mean I'm a big girl. I just wish you would have just told me that you didn't want to be in a relationship. I honestly wish you hadn't took me shopping and bought me gifts. I hate to admit it, but I did kind of feel special. Like you wanted something from me. Like you wanted to be in a committed relationship, but I guess not. I guess because Q is serious about Starr, I had felt like you could be serious about me."

"I'm not saying I can't be serious about you, but Q is so much older than me. It's time that nigga settle down but I'm not there yet. I'm a young nigga."

Jada nodded her head in agreement with him and said, "You're right."

"Look, I like you a lot and I love chilling with you but the timing is not right."

"No need to explain." Jada stood and she felt like a damn fool. For the first time in a very long time, she liked someone and not because they had money. She liked being around Fresh. She was attracted to him and she had let her guard down. She had exposed her heart and it felt like he took a sledgehammer and crushed her heart. She tried to hold back the tears but they came streaming down her face. He stood and embraced her and held her for a very long time. He attempted to kiss her but she pushed him back.

"I have to go," she said.

Chapter 11

JADA CALLED BLACK AND HE ANSWERED ON THE SECOND RING, "Hello?"

"I think I heard something. You need to come over right now and crash on my sofa."

"Are you fucking crazy? It's two in the morning."

"Come on, Black. You got me in this bullshit, so you need to come on over here."

"Why don't you call Fresh? I 'm sure he's in town."

"Fuck Fresh."

"What happened between you?"

"I don't feel like getting into it."

"Okay, give me an hour. I gotta drive all the way over from Cobb."

"An hour? You need to get over here before an hour."

An hour later Black came over. Jada passed him a blanket and a pillow and he fell asleep on the couch. The next morning, Jada had prepared him some breakfast: toast, eggs, grits and bacon.

Black said, "Damn, girl, you can burn."

Jada looked at his silly ass and said, "Well it's just grits and eggs. Who in the hell can't cook that?"

"You'd be surprised."

"Well, if your girl can't cook you some grits, eggs and bacon, you need a new girl."

He was laughing his ass off and stuffing his face at the same time. Black said, "You know I be going to see Shamari."

"You mentioned it."

"And the man really thought I was fucking you."

Jada sighed and ate a spoonful of grits. "Yeah, he asked me about that too and I didn't even want to approach you with that silly-ass shit."

"That's what I told him. I said me and Jada are like brother and sister." Though Black never stared at his sister's ass and lusted. Never jerked off to his sister all of which he had done, while thinking about Jada. Even right now he was looking at her nipple print. He chomped on a slice of bacon and added grape jam to his toast.

"I ain't thinking about Shamari's ass."

"He wanted me to tell him if I knew who you were talking to. I told him I didn't. He said that you had told him that you had a man."

"I told him I was seeing somebody. I didn't tell him I had a man."

"That's the last thing a nigga in jail wants to hear."

"I know, but it was the truth."

"So you and Fresh together?"

"Naw, that ain't working out. I'm surprised he didn't tell you."

"I haven't spoken to him in a while."

"Yeah, he's just like the rest of these dudes. Wants to run around and have multiple women in every city."

"One thing about you is that you will always land on your feet."

"Land on my feet? I don't need a man to be on my feet. I ain't never been off my feet."

Black laughed still chomping on the toast. .

"So where are you going to put me up?" Jada asked.

"Me put you up? You just said that you were on your feet."

"Look, Black, it's your fault that I'm going to have to move in the first place. Why should I have to spend my own money?"

"So what are you looking for? The first month's rent and deposit?"

"Actually, I was thinking of buying something."

"Look, I can't help you with that."

"I know, well just give me six month's rent and we'll be even."

"Six month's rent? You're out of your mind."

"Look, I have to pay a penalty for breaking the lease."

"How much is your rent here?"

"Twenty-five hundred dollars a month."

"Let me think about it."

"Cool."

Chapter 12

Q WAS IN THE SHOWER WHEN ONE OF HIS PHONES RANG. STARR yelled to Q, "Baby, your phone is ringing."

"Get it for me."

Starr answered the phone. "Hello?"

A woman's voice said, "Hello? Is this Quentin's phone?"

"Yeah, this is his girlfriend."

Silence.

"Would you like to speak to him?"

"No, never mind." The woman terminated the call and Starr sat the phone back on the nightstand.

Five minutes later, Q got out of the shower and toweled off and entered the bedroom. Starr was lying on the bed and he said, "Who was that?"

"That was some woman and when I said I was your girlfriend, she appeared to be surprised."

"What?"

Q picked the phone up from the nightstand and dialed the number back. No answer. It was a Houston number. He dialed it again. Still no answer.

"Hmm. that's funny."

"I didn't think it was funny at all."

"What?"

"I didn't think that shit was funny at all. You're just like your boy, Fresh. You think cuz you got all that money that you can just do people any kind of way, but I'm here to let you know, Quentin, I have my own money and

I just don't have to put up with your bullshit."

He looked confused as hell. "Okay, help me understand what's going on in your head. I asked you to answer the phone. You answered the phone and a woman was on the other end of the phone. I have had this number for years. So lots of people know the number. If I had something to hide, do you think I would have let you answer my phone?"

She thought about what he was saying and he was making a good case for himself. If he was hiding something, he certainly wouldn't have let her answer his phone.

"Look, I'm nothing like Fresh. I'm a grown man. Not a game player."

"Why the fuck did she hang up the phone?"

"I don't know why she hung up the phone. Hell, I don't even know who that was."

He tossed her his phone. "Look through my phone. I have nothing to hide. No text from women, no pictures, just text from my kids. I only talk to you, my mom and my kids on that phone. Only people I text is my kids. I don't have all these women throwing theirselves at my feet. Did I used to be a womanizer? Hell yeah, that was me but I swear to you, that's not me now. I'm telling you the truth and that's all I can do. If you don't believe me, that's your problem."

She stood from the bed and was heading toward the door when he grabbed her by the shoulder and stopped her. "Don't leave."

"Look, Quentin, I don't believe you."

He embraced her and said, "Look, I know you've been hurt before but I won't hurt you."

"Can you please let me go?"

He released her and stepped aside. Starr made her way out the door.

Chapter 13

WHEN BLACK ENTERED HIS HOME, HE HEARD AVANT YELLING, "HELP. Help. Help." Black made his way down to the bottom of the stairs. Avant was lying on the dirt floor of the cage. His ribs protruded from his stomach and he looked famished. The basement reeked of pungent shit. He was naked except for one sock.

"I need some water, bruh. I need water."

Black realized that the man hadn't eaten or drank anything since the day that L left, over five days ago.

Black said hold on and then he entered the kitchen. There was nothing inside the fridge but a couple of rotten apples. He opened the cabinet and removed a can of chicken. He opened it and placed it in a bowl. Then he made a glass of ice water and warmed up a packet of Ramen noodles. It wasn't a gourmet meal but at least Avant wouldn't be starving.

When Black opened the cage and presented the meal to him, Avant crawled over to the other side of the cage. Black closed the cage and Avant glanced up at Black. And though he despised Black and thought that Black was Satan in the flesh, he thanked Black for giving him this meal to eat.

Black locked the cage and said, "I got good news for you."

Avant was devouring those Ramen noodles like a hungry Ethiopian. Knowing Black, it would definitely be the last meal that he would have in a while.

Black was grinning. "Don't you want to hear the good news?"

"If you're not letting me go, then I don't care."

"Well, you won't be getting raped anymore. L got murdered."

"What?"

"Got killed in a robbery."

Avant didn't know whether to be thankful or sad. He was glad that he wouldn't be getting his asshole thrashed, but he also had sense enough to know that L would have brought him food. The last time he saw L, he had told Avant that he wasn't going to be around anymore. L had told Avant that he and Black had a disagreement, but Avant really didn't believe him. He and Black had fallen out plenty of times.

Black smiled and said, "So it's going to be me and you."

"Just kill me, bruh."

"That's too easy."

"I killed the only thing that you ever loved, so just finish me off. Please finish me off. I can't take this shit."

"Look, I do what the fuck I want to do."

"What is the purpose of this?"

Black made his way over to the cage and pressed his face against the cage and said, "I'm going to torture your punk ass for the rest of your life."

* • • •

Black was at the stop sign about to exit the neighborhood when a little white boy about ten years old approached his car. The kid had brown matted hair and freckles sprinkled his tiny red face. Black lowered the window.

"Mister, can you help me and my mom? We're having car trouble."

Black removed a fifty-dollar bill from his pocket and said, "Here, take a taxi. I don't have time."

The kid held the money for a second then offered it back and said, "We need help, not money."

"Ryder, what are you doing?" A woman's voice called out.

Black looked up to see a gorgeous white woman in some very form-fitting jeans and a low-cut blouse. She was tanned with a long blonde mane. She was walking fast, approaching Ryder. Ryder turned to face his Mom.

"Mom, I was just asking for help."

Black made eye contact with the Mom and noticed that she had sparkling green eyes and no wedding band and she looked very exotic. Black wondered how Ryder would feel about having a black stepdad.

Black pulled over to the side of the road and hopped out of the car. He grinned at the fine-ass white woman and said, "Ryder was just telling me that you were having car trouble. Where is the car?"

"Well, the car is right around the corner. But if you can let me use your cell phone I would appreciate it. My phone is dead and Ryder left his at home."

"Because you took my phone away," Ryder said.

"Let me look at the car. Maybe I can help. What kind of car is it?"

"A Honda Accord." Then she extended her hand. "I'm Susanne."

"I'm Tyrann."

"Like Tyrann Mathieu?"

"Who?"

Susanne laughed and said, "You must not watch sports. Tyrann Mathieu is a football player."

Black said, "No, I don't have time to watch sports."

Susanne led Black to the blue Honda Accord. She got behind the wheel and fired up the ignition but it wouldn't crank.

Black said, "It sounds like your battery. Do you have any cables?"

"I do. They're in the trunk."

"Get them and I'll pull up and give you a boost. Then you can be on your way."

She smiled seductively at him and said, "You're so nice."

Black nodded, wondering what was under those jeans. Did she give good head? Was she a freak? He hadn't fucked a white girl in quite a long time and it was time to quench that thirst again. He walked slowly to his car. Wondering how he was going to ask her for her phone number. He had to be strategic. He'd told her that he didn't watch sports. The bitch liked football. He would lie to her like he had season tickets to the Falcons game and that she and Ryder could use them if they wanted. It was all planned out.

He drove around the corner to the Accord and hopped out of his car. He hooked the cables up and when she was behind the wheel of the car, a van approached and two huge skinheads with tattoos jumped out of the van and rushed Black. Black stepped back and punched the fuck out of one of them on the side of the jaw. The other man grabbed Black around his waist. By that time, the first man had regained his composure and grabbed Black around his neck.

Black looked at Susanne and said, "Help me!"

The bitch avoided eye contact with him. A third man appeared and he was bigger than the first two. He had a red beard and was wearing overalls. He looked like he spent his afternoons hunting deer.

He said, "You piece of shit nigger, we're going to kill you!"

Black struggled to break free but the three men were too strong for him. He was hoping someone would see him. He would scream for help, but there were no cars on the road at that time of morning. Even if there were, he couldn't scream. Red Beard had covered his mouth. They tossed Black in the back of the van and clocked him upside his head with a stick made of oak and knocked him unconscious. They sped away and headed to a remote location outside of Atlanta.

*. • •

Red Beard slapped the fuck out of Black and woke him up. The men sat Black up in the back of the van and they drug him out of the van into an abandoned warehouse.

"Tell me what the fuck is going on? I don't know you," Black said.

"You don't and we don't know you. We were hired to do a job and that's what we're going to do."

Black wondered what the fuck was going on. He knew he had enemies but who in the hell were these white men? The first person that came to mind was TeTe, but why? He hadn't done anything to her. It wasn't her but who and what the fuck did the man mean by he was paid to do a job?

Red Beard and one of the skinheads approached Black. Black could see the other one out of the corner of this eye. He had some kind of hammer in his hand. Not quit a sledgehammer but perhaps a size down and he was pounding it on the cement floor. Black was afraid. What the fuck were they going to do to him? He kept watching the skinhead with the tattoos pounding that hammer. Were they going to torture him? They were going to kill his ass for sure. His cell phone was in his pocket, if he could only pocket dial someone. At least if they were going to kill him, someone would hear.

Red Beard and skinhead number one grabbed his arm right below his shoulders. Black was still struggling and this pissed Red Beard off.

The white man slapped the fuck out of Black and said, "Quit squirming."

But Black was not about to stop. If they were going to kill him, he was not going out without a fight.

The skinhead with the tats was still playing with that sledgehammer, breaking big chunks of cement with it. He set the hammer down and approached Black from behind, helping the other two restrain him but Black kept putting up a fight.

"Get the fuck off me!" Black yelled.

Red Beard was laughing his ass off and he said, "You think just because you said get the fuck off you, we're going to do what you say? You see Black, it don't work like that. You're going to do what the fuck we say."

Black stopped yelling, wondering, how they knew his name. Not just his name, but his nickname.

The skinhead that had been pounding the pavement with the sledgehammer removed a Taurus 9.mm and said, "Let's just shoot the motherfucker. Let's kill his ass right now and not even worry about it. Let's shoot him and feed his body to the gators. Man, better yet, let's hang the motherfucker. Let's hang his black ass and make it look like a suicide. Nobody will give a damn."

"What the fuck do you want from me?" Black said.

Redbeard approached Black and they were nose to nose. They were so close that Black could smell the tobacco the man had been chewing earlier in the day.

"We are going to need you to stay the fuck away from Sasha Anderson or else."

"That's my business partner."

"She used to be your business partner."

Red Beard and skinhead number one lassoed Black's legs together and removed his shoes. The other skinhead ran back to the sledgehammer before making his way back over to Black and said, "You're going to stay away from her, right?"

Black was nobody's punk but there was no way that he wanted this man to smash his goddamned toes with that hammer. He said, "Look, I'll do whatever you want me to do."

Red Beard said, "Of course you will or the next time it will be Nana's old ass in here."

"Look, man, whatever you need me to do, bruh. Just don't smash my toes with that damn hammer."

"Untie the nigger," Red Beard said. The three men stripped Black butt naked and dropped him off in the middle of a busy intersection in Atlanta.

* • •

Later that night at Sasha's house, over shots of Ciroc, he told her about the big white boys abducting him.

Black downed this liquor and said, "I swear to you. They were some big redneck white boys. I'm not talking about some little pussy-ass white boys that have gone to Catholic school. These were some big motherfuckers. MMA fighters or some shit."

Sasha laughed and said, "I don't believe you, bae. Why are you making this shit up?" She laughed again and it annoyed Black. Then she said, "So these big white boys kidnapped you and told you to stay away from me?"

"I swear it. They told me to stay away, man. They told me they were going to fuck me up."

"But you're here."

"Look, nobody is going to punk me. My Nana will tell you. I'm a hard-headed motherfucker."

She laughed and said, "This is unbelievable. Why would someone tell you to stay away from me? Who even knows that I fuck around with you unless..."

"Unless what?"

"He heard you."

"What do you mean?"

"The other day you were here. I heard your phone ring when he—" She didn't want to relive that moment or any moment that her father had touched her.

"You don't have to say it." Black knew it was hard for her to talk about it.

She looked like she was about to cry and Black hugged her and said, "I promise you. I'm going to take you away from all of this. I swear to God I will kill that motherfucker."

"You can't kill the mayor of the city. You're going to end up in prison for life. I'm going to be all right."

Black stared at her. He couldn't believe that she was defending this motherfucker. This monster had raped her ever since she was a kid. And now he was thinking that was probably the motherfucker that sent those dirty white boys to fuck him up.

Black turned from her gaze and said, "I have a feeling that going to prison for the rest of my life is going to be my fate."

"Don't say that."

"No, don't you say that you're going to be all right. It is not all right what he is doing to you. This shit is not okay and if I witness that shit again, I'm telling you I am going to kill that motherfucka. I am going to kill him. You don't deserve this. You deserve better. This shit ain't normal. A daddy don't fuck his daughter."

She covered her face with her hands and began to cry. He approached her and wrapped his arms around her.

"Look, I'm going to take you away from all this."

"It's not that simple."

"Why ain't it that simple? I want you to get your things and leave."

She uncovered her eyes and her eyes were misty and she said, "It's okay."

"It's not okay. Why do you keep saying that?" He made his way into the bathroom to take a piss and when he returned, she was butt naked.

He was confused. "We were just talking about some real shit and you're naked?"

"Look, babe, just like you believe that your fate is jail. This is my fate."

"Being daddy's mistress?"

She unbuttoned his pants and took him deep into her mouth, gagging on his dick. Before long he was turned on and she pulled his torso toward her mouth and he humped her mouth. She sucked his balls and he plopped down on the sofa. She turned him over on his stomach and licked his asshole.

He tightened up and she said, "Relax. It's going to be okay." She was pleasuring him and he was enjoying it and he was disgusted at the same time. This woman was smart, but she would never be normal. He stopped her and turned over to face her.

She made a sad face. "What's wrong?"

"Nothing is wrong. Get on top."

His dick was rock solid and dripping with saliva. He thought about the condom in his wallet. He didn't need any more goddamned kids. "Wait a minute. Let me get my wallet."

"Your wallet?"

"A condom."

"Just put it in." She straddled him and he slid it in. She used her hands to brace herself and rode him until he exploded inside of her. She hopped up and she licked the cum from the tip of his penis.

He was drained. He made his way into her linen closet to get a towel to clean himself up. When he looked down, he spotted an open suitcase full of cash and checks. Checks made out to the Wasco Corporation.

"Sasha, come here."

She approached him, wrapping her arms around him.

He turned and said, "Whose cash is this and whose checks are these? Why are they here? What the fuck is the Wasco Corporation?"

"It's mine." She released him.

"You're lying."

"What?"

"I can tell when someone is lying. And you're lying."

She turned from his gaze.

"Whose money is this? I'm going to ask you one more motherfuckin' time. Whose money is this?"

She began to cry.

"Bitch, who are you holding this money for and what the fuck is the Wasco Corporation?"

"Look, you need to quit calling me a bitch."

"What is going on?"

"It's his money."

"His? Who is he?"

"Daddy. Wasco is a shell company. You know a place where he hides money."

"Look, I know what the fuck a shell company is."

"He's been taking bribes. That's how he makes money. He does favors for special interest people. For example, if someone wants to build something and there's a zone restriction, he makes sure that they can do it. Some give him bags of cash and others give him checks."

"What?"

"Yes. I'm telling you the truth, Black. Some of these guys are organized crime; actually one man was even accused of being associated with ISIS. The news did a special on him a few weeks ago. I recognized the guy because I'd met him a few times and he'd give me big bags of cash."

"What's his name?"

"Abu Something. I can't remember his name."

"You can't remember his name?"

"No. look, you don't want to ask too many questions. I don't want you end up dead." Her face became serious. " My Daddy will have you murdered. Those men that snatched you up. They are professional killers. They kill people for him."

"Are you serious."

"Very serious."

"But you didn't believe that they kidnapped me."

"I was pretending not to believe you.

"Damn this is crazy!"

"I know."

"Damn, so why didn't your dad give you money to help you with your business?"

"I've already told you. He's stingy and greedy."

"So that motherfucker ain't no better than me. In fact he's worse than me. Everybody has their secrets I guess."

"Yes. Everybody, but that's what I love about you. What you see is what you get."

"You can say that again."

Black took a five-minute shower and toweled off. She was brushing her teeth while he was applying some coconut oil to his skin. Still thinking about that corrupt-ass mayor, thinking about approaching him and treating him. That motherfucker was sure to get his day and Black was going to make sure of it somehow.

Chapter 14

BLACK VISITED SHAMARI AND THE TWO MEN HUGGED BEFORE SITTING down at the table. Black said, "This is cool. Now that I got the fake ID, I'll come see you more often."

"I could have been gotten you an ID earlier, but I had no idea that you would come see me."

"You're my brother, man."

"How is your pops?"

"Cool, still talking shit. He asked me about you. You know he couldn't pronounce your name."

They were both laughing their asses off.

Then Shamari got serious and said, "Do you ever think about Lani?"

"All the time."

"You know it's weird but Lani was in my dream."

"Oh yeah?"

"Well, it wasn't about her. It was about Jada, but Lani was in it. It just goes to show you that Lani is not dead."

"What do you mean?"

"I mean she's dead in this world but I believe that the soul can never die. She's in another world. Can you remember a time when you weren't alive?"

"No."

"That's because you've always been alive. We all have. Our consciousness always has and always will be here."

Black smiled. "Damn. I never really thought about it like that. Yeah, I can believe it, bruh." He shook his head. "You know, we weren't on the best of terms when she died. She wasn't speaking to me and I never had a chance to make things right between us, but her mom and I did make it right."

"Oh yeah, she thought you had her murdered."

"Yeah and that shit was ridiculous. I would never do anything like that. I loved that woman. You knew I loved her and everybody knew I loved her."

"Yeah. I knew that. So what brings you here?"

"Look, I got a way to get you out."

"How?"

"I got some information."

"You want me to rat?"

"Look, it's the mayor. I don't know if I told you his daughter is my business partner."

"Yeah, with the restaurants, right?"

"Yeah. Well anyway, the motherfucker has been accepting bribes and he's had people murdered who was going to come forward and tell on him."

Shamari's eyes lit up. "You think that kind of information will get me out of jail?"

"Murder. This motherfucker has had people murdered. He's the mayor. Of course, you can get out."

"Look, man, I care about my reputation."

"This man doesn't care about nobody. He says that he's going to have me arrested if it's the last thing he does. He has a vendetta against me."

"Look, I'll do anything to help you. You helped me so I'll help you," Shamari said.

"This is the same motherfucker who stood up in the press conference with the DEA and wanted to take us down, remember?" Black said.

"Yeah, I remember," Shamari said.

"Look, man, we gotta get you out of here."

"I'm ready to leave. I hate this goddamn place."

"I'm going to get her to tell me all about the murders, and you can call the Feds and let them know what's up."

"I appreciate you, bruh."

Chapter 15

TERRELL TEXTED STARR: I REALLY LIKE THE TV. YOU WERE RIGHT I needed to upgrade the TV. He was speaking of the television that she had bought without his permission and put in his man cave.

Starr: *I'm glad you like it. I told you that you would like it.*

Terrell: *That's not all I like.*

Starr: *What are you talking about?*

Terrell: *You know what I'm talking about.*

Starr: *:-)*

Terrell: *Does that mean you like me?*

Starr: *I don't mix business with personal.*

Terrell: *I thought you were going to say something about that cornball man of yours.*

Starr: *What makes you think he's a cornball?*

Terrell: *Because he has you working.*

Starr: *Actually, I don't have to work now. I choose to work. I love what I do.*

Terrell: *What's going on in the relationship? Must not be working out for you.*

Starr: *What make you say that?*

Terrell: *Am I right?*

Starr: *Slow down. You going way too far.*

Terrell: *I ain't going far enough.*

Starr: *Look, Terrell, I'm going to see you in a couple of days and you can pay me for my work.*

Terrell: *Let's go to Dubai.*

Starr: *You think you can impress me by taking me to Dubai? Like every thot on Instagram.*

Terrell: *Not impressed?*

Starr: *Not at all.*

Terrell: *I guess you've been to Dubai?*

Starr: *Nope and don't want to go. Now if you're taking about the French Rivera or Monaco, count me in.*

Terrell: *Let's go.*

Starr: *I can't go.*

Terrell: *Must be a special man.*

Starr: *He is.* Even though Starr had her suspicions about Q, she wasn't about to let Terrell think he could take his place. She loved Q and that hadn't changed. She just introduced him to the family and they all loved him.

Terrell: *You can't knock a brother for trying.*

Starr: *I can't. :-) Can you wire transfer the balance. It would be easier for me*

Terrell: *Ok. I'll do that tomorrow.*

Starr: *Good night, Terrell.*

•   •   •

The next day, Starr and Brooke was rearranging the showroom when Terrell walked in wearing a fitted polo shirt and jeans and smelled of Tom Ford cologne that was making her panties very wet. Damn he smelled delicious. Starr had to admit the man was a gorgeous motherfucker. "Mr. Michaels."

He smiled and said, "Why are you so formal, Ms. Coleman?"

"You're a customer."

"I thought we were on a first-name basis."

"You did?" She glanced at Brooke. "What made you think that?"

"Look, I'm just kidding."

"What brings you here?"

"I brought the check."

"Oh, I thought we agreed you would do a wire transfer."

"We did, but since I was in the neighborhood, I thought I would stop by."

Starr gave Brooke instructions on what to do next and she and Terrell excused themselves into the office. He sat down right across from her. He passed her the check.

She glanced at the check before saying, "You made a mistake."

"How?"

"You gave me too much money, about ten thousand dollars too much."

"I didn't accept the discount. You're a hard-working sistah. A single parent at that, so it didn't feel right taking the discount. And the extra seven thousand dollars is a bonus. You deserve it. Though I want you to tell T.J. he is going to have to pay me for my lamp."

She laughed and said, "I don't know what to say. I mean, thank you. Thank you so much, but...well I hope you weren't expecting anything in return."

His hands were resting on the desk and she noticed his manicure. Those damn hands and feet were so big that she knew his fine ass had to have a big dick. She hated that she was looking at him that way but, damn, she couldn't help herself. She knew that he knew what he was doing coming in here and smiling with those sparkling white teeth, She had to keep in mind that even though she and Q were not speaking right now, she would be a good girl.

He glanced at his watch and said, "Well, actually, I was hoping that we could do lunch."

"What?"

"It's almost lunchtime. We don't have to go nowhere fancy. We can go to Boones, its a steakhouse. It's up on Piedmont."

"Yeah, I know where it is."

She looked at her watch then her phone buzzed. It was Q. She quickly sent him to voicemail and then said, "Ok. I'll go to lunch but it will have to be a quick lunch. I have things to do."

He smiled and said, "You're treating, right?"

"What?"

"I'm just kidding."

"Look I'll buy lunch since you were nice enough to give me the bonus. I really do appreciate that."

They sat in the front of the restaurant and she ordered some food. He just ordered water with lemon.

Starr frowned and said, "So you're not going to eat?"

"No, I've eaten already."

"But I'm supposed to pay for your meal."

"You know I was just kidding, right?"

"So what did you have for lunch?"

"A protein shake."

"Yuck."

"It was delicious. It had strawberries, blueberries and plain Greek yogurt. Actually, I would rather eat what you're eating, but when I retired, I was diagnosed with high blood pressure. I was only thirty years old and I was shocked as hell. Here I am, a former pro athlete and still in shape. I play ball a few times a week but I had high blood pressure because I was eating everything that wasn't nailed down. I want to live for a while to enjoy my money."

"I know that's right."

Starr sipped her water and she was clearly wondering what his motive was. What did he want with her? She knew that he would fuck her—he was a man. But she was not about to fuck someone that she couldn't at least see herself having a future with. Not at her age.

"I know you probably want to know why we're here."

"I am."

"Well I wanted to know if you would be interested in working with me."

"In what capacity?"

He laughed and said, "Calm down."

"I'm calm. Trust me." She rolled her eyes.

"Hold on. I think you might have the wrong idea about me. You must think I was brought up as some sheltered motherfucka with a silver spoon in my mouth. I grew up in the south side of Chicago. Got two uncles and a brother doing life in prison."

"What does that have to do with anything?"

"I don't know. I just get this vibe that you think I'm some stuck-up, uppity-ass nigga."

She laughed said, "Would you calm down? I don't know how you read all that from what I said. You were talking about us working together."

"Yeah. You know I'm in real estate?"

"You mentioned it."

"I have been offered a reality show and I want you to come in occasionally when I give open houses and decorate."

"I don't want to be on a reality show. I'm a low profile kind of girl. I don't need everybody knowing me."

"Well, it will be just a guest appearance."

"Now, why would I want to do that? What's in it for me?"

"More business."

"I don't want to get more business. I just want the right kind of customer."

"What is the right kind of customer?"

"Not a petty-ass, nickel-and-dime person that complains about the price."

"Well, don't you see? Here is the chance to brand yourself. You get famous—"

"I don't want fame. I told you that."

"Well, once you get your name out there, you can be more selective with your customers."

He had made a good point but while she did want the business, she wanted to be able to go to the mall without everyone pointing and asking if she was the girl from the reality show. Then she had to think about her son. She didn't want people all in his life.

"I'm going to have to think about it. Can I get back with you on that later?"

"Take your time. Think about it and let me know, but I just want to say, I would love for you to be on the show."

"I'm going to think about it."

He said, "I bet you thought I was going to hit on you, didn't you?"

"Actually, I didn't know what to expect."

"I do like you a lot. But I respect our relationship."

"Good, besides, this is Atlanta. There are lots of good professional women out there."

"I want you."

"You don't know me."

"I want what I see. Unless you're telling me that what you see is not what you get."

"I'm just like every other female out there. I have good and bad days. I can be a bitch. I can be moody and I can be slightly possessive and obsessive and bipolar and jealous about somebody I love."

"You love hard?"

"Extremely."

"Me too."

"I don't know if that's a good thing or bad thing," she said.

"But you're bipolar?"

"I didn't say I was bipolar. I said I can be bipolar and what's wrong with being bipolar anyway? I think nothing is wrong with being bipolar if you're getting help. Black people put a stigma on mental illness and that leads so many people that need help not to seek it."

"You're right. But just for you saying that lets me know that you're very intelligent and that's what I want. Somebody slightly hood with intelligence."

She laughed and said, "I'm slightly hood with intelligence?"

"I think so."

"Well, I'm actually more than slightly, but am I going to be acting ratchet when I'm doing business? Hell no."

"And that's why you need to think about doing the reality show. There will be a lot of girls rooting for you. A lot of girls out there in the hood that you can inspire to do better."

"I'll think about it."

Chapter 16

THE CONCIERGE PHONED Q TO LET HIM KNOW THAT MR. DIEGO Gonzales was there to see him.

"Who?"

"Diego Gonzales."

"Tell him that I'm coming down."

Q had thought the concierge had to be mistaken when he said Diego Gonzales. What the fuck was he doing here and the nerve of this motherfucker for coming to his house. He wanted to kill this dude. Q slipped on his shoes and took the elevator to the lobby where he found a grinning-ass Diego talking to the concierge. The man was handing Diego some literature about the building. It appeared that he was inquiring about buying a place in the building. Diego thanked the concierge and approached Q.

Q led him to the furnishings in the middle of the lobby and when they were seated, Q asked, "What the fuck are you doing here?"

"I'm thinking about buying a place in your building. This is a very nice building."

"What the fuck are you doing in Atlanta?"

"I didn't know I had to have permission from you to travel to Atlanta."

"You're lucky I don't kill your punk ass up in here."

"You're too smart for that."

"What the fuck do you want?"

"I want us to start working again."

"Are you out of yo mind?"

Diego laughed, flashing some horsey-ass veneers. He'd gotten some bad dental work in Mexico since the last time Q had saw him.

"I want to pay you back for the bad coke," Diego said.

"What part of 'we'll never work together again', don't you understand. I am not fuckin' with you, dude. Never again in life." Q stood and said, "As a matter of fact, get the fuck out or I will have you escorted out."

Diego smiled again with those square-ass chicklet teeth. Those were the biggest goddamned teeth Q had ever seen. He stood and made his way toward the exit just before he asked, "How are the amenities?"

• • •

TeTe called Jada and she picked up on the second ring.

TeTe said, "Still looking for a place?"

"Yes."

"I have a townhouse that's in Sandy Springs that you can move into if you want to. It's really nice. I usually rent it for twenty-four hundred a month but I'll give it to you for fifteen since you are family."

"I'm family?" Jada laughed.

"Well, when I say that it just means that I like you. That's all."

"I really don't want to be out in Sandy Springs. But I'll take a look at it."

"Where are you trying to be?"

"You know I want to be near Buckhead. Somewhere where the action is."

"Okay, let's meet and look at the place and if you don't like it, I'll hook you up with my realtor. She rents properties too."

"Text me the address of the house in Sandy Springs."

Two hours later, Jada wasn't in love with the townhouse in Sandy Springs. It was roomy but it had carpet and she preferred hardwood floors and the bathroom was just so-so. After TeTe finished showing her the home, they decided to grab a quick bite to eat at the Panera Bread Company at the Perimeter Center.

Both women had a salad. TeTe had water and Jada ordered green tea. As soon as they were seated, TeTe's phone rang. A call from an unfamiliar number. After three rings she answered.

"Hello?"

"Hey, it's Cassandra."

Cassandra? TeTe was staring at the ceiling trying to think. Who the fuck was Cassandra? She knew all of her girls by name. She had just hired a new girl but her name was Roxie, not Cassandra. TeTe said, "I don't know no goddamned Cassandra."

"You remember I met you and Black at the Waffle House?" Then it dawned on her that Cassandra was the tranny. She'd called a week ago looking for Black. TeTe had forgotten to save her number. Black had told her that his friend L had gotten murdered and TeTe wondered what the fuck did she want now.

"Look, I thought you had Black's number."

"No, this ain't about Black. I want to see you."

TeTe sat her water down and said, "Why do you need to see me?"

"Remember I was telling you about the girl that I had that we called Miss America?"

"Yeah. You have a picture of her that you can send?"

"Yeah, but she's with me now and if you want, we can come see you now."

"I'm out in Sandy Springs."

"That's cool because we're in Roswell."

"We're at Panera Bread at the Perimeter Center."

"Okay, we'll see you in fifteen minutes."

"Cool." TeTe terminated the call and said, "We're going to have company in a minute."

"Who?"

"A couple of he-she's."

"What?"

"I'm going to put one of them to work. If she looks hot."

"What do you mean?"

"Exactly what I said. I'm going to put the bitch to work if she's hot."

"You got a market for them?"

"You'd be surprised. Men that you think are straight ain't so straight. I'm talking about businessmen to dope boys. This is Atlanta—anything goes."

"I don't get it. Who would want to fuck with someone that looks like a woman? Why not get a real woman. I mean there are enough tranny-looking real bitches around here."

"Hey, look I'm a business lady. I'm not trying to be somebody's psyche."

Jada was laughing her ass off at TeTe.

TeTe's phone rang. "Hello?"

"I'm looking for you. I don't see you."

TeTe looked toward the door and spotted Fy-Head and the other woman. She waved them over and when they got closer TeTe realized that there was no possible way that she could tell that Miss America was a man. Unlike Fy-Head, she had smooth skin, soft looking hands and a curvaceous figure as well as an ass that made Jada's look basic. The makeup was overdone but that was to be expected.

Jada said, "Goddamn! The tall one is gorgeous."

They sat in the booth and TeTe extended her hands to both of them. Jada looked at Fy-Head and could tell right away he was a man. The makeup covered razor bumps, but even he had a knock out body.

TeTe said, "What is your real name, Miss America? I mean I'm not going to be calling you Miss America."

"Just call me Rachel. My government name is Raymond, but I've been going by Rachel since I was twelve."

"Twelve?" Jada asked.

"Yeah, that's when I knew I couldn't go on pretending that I was a boy. I'd been hearing the whole time that God doesn't make mistakes and that I was a boy and I should stop acting like a girl."

"God don't make mistakes. If you were born a boy, you're boy," Jada said.

Fy-head said, "Who the fuck made you the moral authority over gender issues?"

"Who the fuck do you think you're talking to?"

"I'm talking to you, fish," Fy-Head stood up and was twirling his neck and some of the patrons were looking on.

Jada said, "You might be a man but I'm telling you, you are fucking with the wrong bitch." Jada was not going to fight this muscle man in a skirt but she would shoot the fuck out of his bitch ass if she felt threatened.

"Calm down, Cassandra. And Jada just be quiet for a minute."

"Yeah, you better make that ho shut up before I shut her up."

Jada was about to say something but TeTe placed her finger over her mouth and said, "Shhh."

TeTe made eye contact with Miss America, "So you're transsexual?"

"No, but I'm transitioning."

"Have you ever done this before?" TeTe asked.

"What?"

"Trick, bitch," Fy-Head said. "You know damn well what she talking about."

"Well, I've gone out with sugar daddies but not like sell pussy for a price."

Jada was laughing her ass off thinking that this ho thinks that she has a pussy.

TeTe said, "Well hell, it's the same thing. You weren't going out with those sugar daddies because you were attracted to them. You were going out with them because you thought you could get something from them."

"Maybe."

"Maybe, my ass." Fy-head said. "TeTe is right."

Jada was staring at Miss America's weave. She had to admit the bitch looked good and that was the same kind of hair that she had. That weave had to cost at least a thousand dollars.

Miss America was tapping her fingernails on the table looking impatient as if TeTe was wasting her time and that she was above what TeTe could possibly offer her.

"Let me explain how it works," TeTe said.

"Please do because I ain't got all day."

TeTe wanted to curse the bitch out for her snotty-ass attitude but she had to remember this was business and now was not the time to get all emotional.

"I get you clients. Well-established businessmen. Athletes, even dope boys. Some don't even want to have sex.

Jada was wondering who in the hell were the dope boys. But she knew everything goes in Atlanta.

"What is the pay?"

"Locally, meaning right around Atlanta, we will make five to ten thousand per night. Internationally, pay starts at thirty thousand per night.

"We?"

"Yeah, whatever you make, you split with me."

Miss America was in deep thought before she said, "Look, if I gotta split with you, I don't want to work unless I'm making at least twenty thousand dollars a month. I got bills to pay."

Fy-Head said, "Damn, you got me thinking about coming out of retirement."

Miss America was flipping that hair over her shoulder and it was annoying the hell out of Jada.

"So when do we start?" she asked.

"This weekend or even tonight. I have clients that need girls every night of the week."

"Let's do Saturday because I have something going on Friday."

"I'm going to need some pictures. They can be fully clothed or lingerie. I also need to know if you are pre-op or post-op."

"Whose fucking business is it? Why do we even need to let them know at all?"

"Do you wanna end up dead?" Fy-Head interjected. "I'm always telling these hoes that you can play that shit with the wrong man. My best friend right now got her jaw broke for that bullshit."

"Nobody can tell that I was born a male. So."

"Duh, if you have a dick, they are going go find out. Don't worry about that. I have men that like that. So just tell me if you're pre-op or post-op?"

"I'm transitioning. I told you."

"So you still have your penis?"

Miss America huffed as if she was annoyed and then she finally said, "Yes. I have it."

"Well, you might have to use it."

"What do you mean, he might have to use it?" Jada said.

"You will be addressing me as a she, bitch."

Jada stood up and said, "Don't make me come across the table on your ass."

TeTe said, "Sit down, Jada. We are almost done." Then she turned to Miss America and said, "Some men will want to fuck you and some will want you to fuck them. Do you have a problem with that?"

"Yuck," Jada said.

Fy-head rolled her eyes at Jada.

Miss America said, "As long as I'm getting paid."

TeTe shook hands with Miss America and said, "Get me those pictures."

Chapter 17

Q CALLED STARR SIXTEEN TIMES OVER A TWO-DAY PERIOD AND SHE finally answered the phone.

He said, "We need to talk."

"There is nothing to talk about."

"Oh, but there is."

She hung up the phone and fifteen minutes later he was in the lobby of her building. She had instructed the concierge to let him come up. When she opened the door, T.J. sprinted up and gave him a hug.

"What's been up, little buddy?"

"Mommy is going to let me take up Tai Kwan Do then I'll be able to fight."

"Man, don't you hurt nobody."

"I'm not going to hurt anybody unless they try to hurt me or Mommy."

Starr said, "That's right."

She kissed him on the cheek and he ran back to play in his room. He'd gotten used to playing in his room when his mother had company. When they heard his door close, she turned to Q.

"So what's up, Q?"

"Just coming to see if you've calmed down."

"I'm always calm."

He sat on the sofa even though she never offered him a seat. She continued to stand, wanting him to leave.

"Let me get this straight. You're mad at me because somebody called? A woman and they didn't say anything. They just hung up the phone."

"Obviously the bitch was looking for you and didn't expect me to answer the phone."

"Yes, that's very obvious. I agree, but how can you blame me because somebody called me? How can you do that? What the fuck?"

She sat down on the sofa and said, "Q, we need to take a break. Just a break and if we get back together, it was meant to be."

"What if I don't want to take a break?"

"It's not about what you want."

He stared at her like she was crazy. She sat on an armchair and grabbed an Essence magazine that was lying on the table and she flipped through some pages. Not really looking at it, but she didn't want to look at him.

"Maybe we should take a break because you have a lot of issues."

She flung the magazine back on the table and said, "I have a lot of issues? What the fuck you mean I have a lot of issues? You are the one with the bitches calling your phone. An almost forty-year-old man that can't get out of the drug game. What the fuck?"

"Look, man, just because you see Fresh do something, don't mean that I'm guilty of it. I ain't did shit and you know it. And just because Trey did you a certain kind of way, don't mean that it should be held against me. I love you, Starr. I love T.J. I was happy to meet your family. I love your mom and I like your pops."

"Ok, just because you met my family don't mean we need to be together."

"I don't think we had an issue until you worked on the basketball player's house. He had something to do with it, didn't he?"

"What? Are you fucking serious? Your gut is telling you that he has something to do with it? You think he made that bitch call your phone? Get the fuck out of here."

"So you want to take a break?"

"Yup."

"I guess you're going to get with the basketball player and if that don't work out, then you'll come running back to me."

"You don't know what the fuck you're talking about."

"So we're taking a break?"

"We're taking a break."

"Ok, cool. We're taking a break then. It's fine with me. I'm telling you now, I'm not going to sit on my hands and wait on you to make up your mind about what you want to do, I mean just because you're unsure about your feelings. Don't play games with me."

"What the hell is that supposed to mean?"

"Exactly what it sounds like."

T.J. came running out of the room and Q stood and hugged him.

T.J. said, "Godfather, will you take me to see a Hawks game?"

"I sure will."

"I'll take you," Starr said.

"He asked me."

"I'm his mom."

"And I'm his godfather. Hawks and Wizards play tonight at eight." He made eye contact with Starr and said, "I will pick him up at seven." Then he exited her apartment.

• • •

Black's baby mama Asia was watching Empire on Hulu while the kids were gone when she heard a knock on the door. "Who is it?"

"The police. Can we talk to you for a minute?"

Fuck, she thought. Why didn't she peek out the blinds? What the fuck did they want?

She opened the door to see two black detectives. The same two clowns that she had lied to about having her car stolen. She knew they were there to question her about Black. She opened the door and let them in. The short perverted officer was staring at her chest and she tightened her house robe.

Kearns said, "Let's get down to business because I know you know why we're here."

"I have an idea," Asia said as she kept her eyes on the pervert that was staring at her tits.

"May we have a seat?"'

"No, you may not."

"You remember a few weeks ago when we came over and told you that your car was at the scene of a crime?"

"Yeah."

"You lied to us, Ms. Stallings."

The pervert had stepped to her side and was now looking at her ass as he licked his chapped ass lips.

"I didn't lie."

"You said your car was stolen."

"It was."

"By who?'

"I don't know."

"Perhaps Tyrann Massey stole it." He paused. "Or maybe you loaned it to him."

"What the fuck are you talking about?"

Kearns presented her with a text exchange between her and Black.

Black: *Bae. How are the kids?*

Asia: *Why don't you come see how they are with your trifling ass?*

Black: *Don't be like that, Bae.*

Asia: *Quit calling me, Bae.*

Black: *Why the hostility? We just saw each other the other night. You said that I was the only one that could fuck you right.*

Asia: *OMG you get on my nerves so bad. WTF do you want?*

Black: *Can I borrow your car?. The Camaro?*

Asia: *Why do you need my car? You have a car.*

Black: *I totaled my car.*

Asia: *Just get a rental.*

Black: *I don't trust rental car companies. They work with the police.*

Asia: *Come and get it but I swear to God, your black ass better not get into shit involving my car.*

Black: *I'll be over when I think the kids are sleep and if you're good, I'll give you some dick.*

Asia: *I ain't fuckin you no more.*

Black: *I've heard that before.*

Asia stood there looking like a goddamned idiot. She couldn't believe that they had her text messages. She couldn't lie her way out of it.

"What do you want from me?

"Cooperation."

"You have the text messages. What else do you need?"

"We need you to say that you loaned Tyrann the car."

"Why?"

"Because if you don't say you loaned him the car, we are going to prove it and then you will be an accessory to murder. Do you want that?"

The pervert had moseyed his way over to an end table where he picked up a digital picture frame with a picture of Asia and two of her girlfriends at Atlantic Station then he turned to Asia. "Hey, this girl right here in the middle? Is this Shaniqua Wright?"

"Yes. Please put down my picture."

"Are you going to play ball or not?"

"How can I be sure that you won't come back and lock me up?"

"We'll give you immunity papers to sign."

"Yes. I loaned him the car."

Chapter 18

TETE AND JADA FOUND A PLACE FOR JADA TO STAY IN BUCKHEAD, BUT Jada would have to stay in a hotel suite for a month until her place was ready.

TeTe said, "As a matter of fact, can you meet me at the Four Seasons? We can get you a place there."

"I can't stay there."

"Why not?"

"I was evicted. I was banned from there a few months ago because the cops showed up with a search warrant."

"I'll get it in my name, since I'm going to pay for it."

"You're going to pay for it and not Black?"

"Yeah, I like you Jada. As a matter of fact, I want you to meet me there and I will give you the keys. Plus the new girl, Miss America, has a client there and I wanted to meet with her there. I always like to be with my girls on the first day."

"Only this girl ain't a girl."

"Hey, maybe not to you but she's a girl to someone."

"I suppose."

Jada and TeTe met in the lobby of the hotel and TeTe passed Jada the key.

"Do you have any clients for the new girl yet?"

"As soon as I put her picture up on the website, I got two businessmen. And someone from Dubai wanted me to send her over because they said that she looked like a woman."

"What the fuck ever."

"See, that's the difference between me and most women. I don't let my personal feelings get in my way of making money."

"So the man in this hotel, he's a businessman?"

"Honestly, I don't know what he does. He said that he'd triple the price of the highest bidder and the highest bidder was ten thousand. The man in Dubai was offering thirty-five thousand, but she said she didn't want to go over there. She said she was scared because some of the foreigners would kill her if they found out that she was actually a he."

"I bet," Jada said. "Look, TeTe, thanks for the room. I'll see you later."

Jada was inside her hotel suite getting settled in when the phone rang. It was Fresh. What the fuck did he want? Why was he calling her? She sent his ass to voicemail. Then he called two more times. She finally answered. "Hello?"

"Jada, I want to talk to you."

"About what? You told me what you wanted. There is nothing to talk about."

"Yes there is. I want to see you. I'm coming over."

"I'm not at home. I'm staying at the Four Seasons until I get my new place."

"You moving?"

"Yes."

"Why?"

"Because I want to."

"Look, your place is five minutes away. I'll be there soon. What room are you in?"

"1946."

"Give me twenty minutes."

"I'll be waiting."

Jada had been lying around in sweatpants and a T-shirt. She hadn't planned on anyone coming over so she wanted to be comfortable. Now that Fresh was bringing his ass over, she would have to slide into something more presentable. She showered, wrapped her hair and slipped into tight black yoga pants that made her ass pop. Let the motherfucker see what he's been missing. Her T-shirt was tied in a strategic knot above her ass designed especially to torment him.

Fresh banged on the door. She opened the door then turned and hurried back to the bed. She could feel his eyes on her. When she was sitting up on the bed she realized that he wasn't behind her.

She said, "Hey, where are you?"

"I'm here. I was just waiting on you to invite me in."

"You're in. Close the door and come have a seat."

He shut the door and moseyed to a chair by the window, parallel to the bed.

"So what's up, Mr. Fresh?" She was trying her best not to think about how good the motherfucker looked right now. She had to keep reminding herself that he had broken her heart.

"I didn't like how the conversation went the other day."

"Are you cold? This room is kind of cold."

"Actually I'm hot, but you can turn on the heat if you want."

"I just got out the shower. Maybe that's why I'm cold." She leaped from the bed and scooted over to the thermostat. She knew he was watching her ass and she liked it. But she told herself she would be good tonight as she sat back on the bed Indian style. She had her blanket up to her knees and settled back on the bed.

"I didn't like how the conversation went the other day," he said again.

She gave him a fake smile and said, "I actually liked the conversation. You told me exactly how you felt and I had to respect that. I didn't like it but I had to respect it."

"What is that supposed to mean?"

"It means exactly what you think it means. I know what you want and you don't want what I want."

He was silent for a moment. He was very reflective and finally he said, "You know what? You were right. I led you on. I knew you wanted more but I thought I told you that I didn't want anything at the time."

"You may have. But when you are showing a girl the attention that you gave me that's what she sees and nothing else."

"I know and I'm sorry for that."

"I don't understand. Why are you here? You could have told me that over the phone."

"The truth is, Jada, I miss you." He sat on the edge of the bed.

"Get back to your corner. Go back over there. Don't come near me."

"It's like that?" He made his way back over to the chair. "Jada, I know I was wrong for bringing that girl around Starr but don't act like you no angel."

"I never said I was an angel. I never claimed to be an angel. I've played a lot of dudes in my day, but I wanted something different from you and I thought we could have something."

"And we still can."

She laughed and said, "Okay, I'm supposed to be that chick that just sit back and wait on you to finished fucking all yo' hoes. And who knows how many hoes you got back in Houston. I'm going to get myself tested. Damn! How could I be so stupid?"

"You're not stupid, Jada. I like you a lot and as far as getting yourself tested, you don't have to do that."

"What? Are you trying to say you didn't fuck that girl?"

"I didn't have sex with that woman."

"Head is sex you know."

"I didn't get any from her." He laughed but then saw that Jada wasn't smiling.

"Are you trying to say that you haven't had sex with nobody else the whole time you been fucking with me?"

"I ain't saying all that but when is the last time you've been tested?"

"Six months ago."

"I'm good. I'm telling you you're wasting your time."

"What kind of nigga shit is that? I'm supposed to believe you?"

"That's not what I'm saying."

"What are you saying?"

"I missed you so much."

"But you don't wanna be with me."

"I don't want to be with anybody. I never meant to have a son. I'm in a dangerous game, Jada. I mean I could get arrested any day or killed. I don't want to have a family or a girlfriend as long as I'm playing this game. So when I felt myself getting close to you, I had to do something so that we slow it down a notch."

Jada picked up a pair of curling irons from the nightstand and flung it toward him barely missing his head. "You should have told me all of this from the beginning. You played with my heart, Fresh. You played with my emotions and I am not a game. I am a person with feelings, you know?"

"I know and I'm sorry."

She began to cry. He got up and sat on the bed. He hugged her and they held each other for a long time. He kissed her neck then her lips. She knew that she should be pushing him away, but she wanted him at the same time. She hated feeling like this. She couldn't resist him. His hand was on her ass and tugging at those tight yoga pants. He stood and dropped his pants. His chocolate stick was bulging through his boxers until he removed them. Then she was staring at it in the flesh.

He removed his shirt and now she was flinging her yoga pants on the floor then the T-shirt came off and she removed the yellow thong. Her nipples were erect and waiting for him to lick and tease them with his lips. He sat on the bed and leaned into her, his hands were on her ass. He fell on his back and she lay on top of him. He pushed his finger inside her VJ. It was wet and she kissed him on his chest before they locked lips. He was still pushing his finger in and out of her pussy. She could feel his stiff chocolate stick press against her leg. His dick was damn hard and she wanted it inside her, but she kissed his chin and then his neck. With her tongue, she licked his chest and moved all the way down to his bellybutton where she circled it with her mouth and then she took him in her mouth. She was licking and sucking. She gripped his dick like she was holding a microphone and then she finally licked the head.

He sighed and was staring at the ceiling thinking about what he'd been missing. Brianna was pretty but she wasn't a complete freak like Jada. Jada was the kind of girl that would always turn him on.

Jada started to licked his balls and he said, "Turn over, baby. I want to be inside you."

She hopped up and disappeared into the bathroom then came back out with a condom and tossed it to him.

He stared at the condom like he was in an Algebra class—confused as hell. "Put it on."

"But you just gave me head."

"I know what I did. Put it on or we're not fucking."

His dick was stiff and pointing toward the ceiling. He ripped open the pack with his teeth and placed it over his dick.

She flipped over on her stomach and he entered her. Slapping those massive ass checks, he gripped her tiny-ass waist and thrust, banging her head against the headboard. She lifted her leg for him and bit down hard on the pillow to keep from screaming. There was nothing worse than being out in the hallway the next day and neighbors from the next room giving you the eye after they heard you getting your brains fucked out.

The next day they were in the restaurant in the lobby and Jada spotted Miss America across the room having breakfast with a client. Jada nudged Fresh and said, "You see that woman on the other side of the room?"

Fresh glanced across the room and spotted the woman. "Yeah."

"What do you think about her? Is she pretty?"

He took a closer look at her. "Not my type."

"What do you mean?"

"I don't wanna wake up with makeup all over my pillow. Bitch looks like she probably takes two hours to dress. One thing I like about you is that your skin is flawless so you don't need all that makeup."

"So she has on too much makeup?"

"Yeah. What's with all the questions? I don't understand. Do you know the bitch or something?"

"That's a man."

"No fuckin way."

"I'm telling you."

He laughed and said, "Were you trying to set me up or something?"

"No, just trying to see if you could tell."

Fresh looked at the woman again and said, "Actually now that you mentioned it, her hands are a little big but other than that, I can't tell at all. How do you know her?"

"I just met her."

"How?"

"My friend TeTe runs an escort service."

"You haven't been an escort before have you?"

"Hell the fuck no!"

"Oh okay. I'm just asking, man." He paused then asked "So the guy that she's with is her client,"

"Exactly."

Chapter 19

TETE WAS SURPRISED TO SEE TODD WHEN SHE OPENED THE DOOR.
She led him into the den and when they were seated she said, "Would
you like water or anything to drink?"

"No."

She studied his face and noticed that he looked very worried. She sat
there waiting on him to say something but he didn't and she finally said,
"Is there something wrong?"

"Actually there is."

"What?"

"Did you kill my cousin?"

"What would make you say that?"

"Look, he was found on the side of the road. Someone had run over him
and just left him on the side of the road."

"And what makes you think it was me? Did someone tell you it was me?"
She maintained eye contact with him without flinching.

"Hey, look. I'm just asking a question."

"And I'm telling you. I didn't kill him."

"Did you have him killed?"

"No."

"The day before he died. I spoke with him on the phone. He said he was
pretty sure you were going to send him to Chicago soon."

"Look, I didn't even know he was dead until I seen it on the news."

"But you never called me to ask me about it. That was a bit strange."

"Look, motherfucka, why are you worried about him anyway? I know that he was your cousin but he was going to rat. He was going to tell on us all." She stood and paced and said, "I know he was your cousin but he was also a stupid motherfucker."

"So you did kill him?"

She stopped pacing and looked Todd in his eyes and said, "What if I did? What the fuck are you going to do about it, Todd? Go running your motherfuckin' mouth like yo cousin?"

"My cousin didn't say shit. You don't know what the fuck he said."

"You're right, I don't know, but the bottom line is he was stupid," TeTe said.

"He was my cousin," Todd yelled. "Do you know what it's like to see my auntie crying because she lost her only son?"

TeTe said, "You know what, Todd? It's time for you to get the fuck out my house before you be seeing your cousin face to face. I never thought it would come down to this. I never thought you would ever be in my face asking me about some bullshit I don't know anything about."

"You don't know anything about? You all but admitted that you had him killed."

"I didn't admit to shit. I don't know what the fuck happened to your cousin," TeTe said and at that moment, she believed her own lies. She had convinced herself that she didn't have anything to do with Dank's murder. And Todd was crazy not her.

"Get the fuck out of my house, Todd. You need to leave and leave right now," she said.

Todd stood up and made his way toward the living room with TeTe trailing him. Just before he exited he turned and said, "You're going to pay for what you done to my cousin."

TeTe wished that she had her gun on her. If she had it on her, she would have surely shot the fuck out of Todd. She said, "Motherfucka, do you know who you are threatening?"

He turned to face her and said, "I'm the one that did all the dirt for you."

"Then who murdered your punk ass cousin?" she asked, as she slammed the door hard.

• • •

A stripper named Sapphire arranged the meeting between Shakur's brothers and Todd, telling them that he had information about who killed Shakur. They would meet at Folley's for Todd's safety. Though he wasn't afraid of the brothers, he really didn't want any problems either. Sapphire was there because she knew everybody involved. She was a curvaceous woman with scarlet colored hair and a tribal sleeve tattoo. She mostly danced at the white clubs, like the Pink Pony and Cheetahs. Once they were all seated, Sapphire made the introduction and Shakur's brothers shook hands with Todd.

Jabril said, "Sapphire told us that you know who killed our brother?"

"I do."

"A nigga named Black, right?"

"No."

Rakeem laughed and said, "This nigga don't know what the fuck he's talking about."

Todd sipped his drink and said, "I'm not saying that Black didn't have anything to do with it, because he did."

Everybody listened in silence and finally Sapphire said, "Is this guy named Tyrann? He drives a Porsche. Is dark skinned with locks?"

Todd said, "Yeah."

Jabril and Rakeem turned to look at her. Rakeem said, "You know him?"

"Every stripper in Atlanta knows him."

"You ever had any dealings with him?"

"You mean have I ever fucked him?"

"Have you?"

"No. Hell no, but I know a lot of bitches that have."

Todd was looking impatient as hell. He wanted to finish telling them what he knew.

Rakeem said, "Can we let the man finish?"

Todd said, "About a month ago, Black's car got shot up and he thought Shakur had something to do with it."

"Wait a minute. I thought you said Black didn't kill my brother?"

"He didn't." He paused and sipped his drink. "There was a woman in the car with Black—his girlfriend."

"What about her?"

"She had your brother killed."

"What? This ain't making no sense."

"Look, the woman's name is TeTe Myers. She runs an escort service here in Atlanta. She had your brother murdered and the reason I know is she came to me and asked me to do it but I said hell no. She wanted to pay me five grand. I told her that wasn't enough." Todd lied. "But she paid my cousin and he did it."

"Your cousin killed my brother?" Jabril said and Todd noted that he was becoming angry at him.

Todd said, "Wait a goddamned minute. You need to lower your voice, partna. I ain't have shit to do with it."

Rakeem said, "He's right."

Jabril said, "I'm sorry."

Rakeem looked confused. "So where the fuck is your cousin? That's who I need to find. "

Todd said, "He's dead. TeTe murdered him."

"Where the fuck is this TeTe bitch?" Jabril said.

"No the biggest question is how do we know you're telling the truth?" Rakeem said.

"Look, there was an article in the newspaper about my cousin. The article was talking about how he was a suspect in your brother's death and how he ended up dead. The police is thinking it was foul play. I mean I don't know how to spell it out for you. She did it."

"What part did Black play in it?"

"I don't know? Perhaps he ordered it."

"How do we get to Black?"

"I don't know."

"Fuck Black! Where does TeTe live?" Jabril said.

"Look, I can tell you where she lives but going to her house is not a good idea."

"Why not?"

"Her neighborhood is exclusive. You'll never make it out of there."

"It's gated?"

"Yes. Nobody is ever at the gate but its heavily patrolled and security pulls people over at random that don't have the community sticker on their car."

Rakeem said, "I don't understand this. Why are you telling us this? Is it because of your cousin?"

"That's exactly why! If my cousin was still living, you wouldn't hear a motherfuckin' word out of me."

"So what's in it for you now? You want us to kill TeTe?"

"I want that bitch to pay and I'm here to help you. Any kind of way that I can."

Chapter 20

WHEN FRESH ENTERED Q'S HOME HE SAID, "I SEEN DIEGO."

Q said, "The motherfucker came over here. Wanted to come up in my place to talk."

"Are you fuckin serious? No way!" Fresh said. He sat down and asked, "Can I have a drink?"

"Water or soda?"

"No, I need something stronger. Give me some vodka. You got any Absolut or Ciroc?"

Q poured Fresh a glass of Grey Goose. It wasn't what he requested but it was all that Q had at the moment.

"Yeah, the nerve of this motherfucker. He wants to do business. Can you believe that?"

"Yes. You know that you were moving most of his work. Why do you think Gordo came looking for you? They know that you can move the work."

"I guess." Q poured himself a shot of liquor. "Have you spoken with Jada?"

Fresh stared at Q and wondered why he'd asked that question. It was a rather odd question. He almost never asked about Jada.

"As a matter of fact, I just left her hotel the other day."

"Her hotel?"

"Yeah, she's moving so she's living in a hotel."

"When did y'all start seeing each other again?"

Fresh laughed and said, "You didn't think she would stay mad at me, did you? We have an understanding now. I told her I didn't want to be in a relationship and she okay with it."

"Whatever. No woman is going to be okay with that situation forever." He sighed. "I'm going through it with Starr right now."

"What do you mean you're going through it with Starr?"

"Somebody called my phone the other night and hung up."

"I'm not understanding."

"It was a woman that called."

"You let Starr answer your phone, bruh?"

"Fuck, yeah. She's my woman. Well, she was my woman."

"And she's tripping?"

"Let's get back to Diego."

"What about him?"

"Part of me wants to get him to bring the work and just take off and move. You know, get him for a couple of thousand kilos."

Fresh laughed. "What's stopping you? This is exactly what we need to be doing."

Q said, "Naw. I have to have him. I got to get him for what he did to Rico. We gotta get him, bruh. We can't let him get away with it"

"And we won't. We can take the work, sell it and divide it between Rico's kids."

"Diego is the kind of motherfucker you have to kill and that's what I intend to do.

Fresh gulped down the liquor then poured him another shot. "And I want to get the money back." He looked Q directly in the eyes and said, "You feel me?"

"I'll never do business with that man. Are you out of your mind?"

"First of all, he owes us."

"Gordo is going to make it right, remember?"

"Quit being a pussy, man. We gotta get this motherfucka."

Q knew what Fresh was saying was right. He owed it to Rico's family to make it right. He had to get even. He had to take Diego out but he wanted to do it his way.

"I'm dealing with Gordo."

"Look, I'll do business with Diego and you continue to work with Gordo. I'm going to get that motherfucker if that's the last thing I do," Fresh said. He then downed his drink and poured another shot.

Q knew there was no use in trying to talk Fresh out of it.

• • •

Jada noticed a man glancing in her direction from the other side of the restaurant. He was exactly her type. Tall. Chocolate. Fine as hell with ultra-white teeth. There was only one thing that she didn't like, the bitch sitting across the booth from him with the tacky-ass blonde weave. She could tell that the man was some kind of hustler by the Prada shoes he was wearing and the fact that he'd knocked over a glass accidentally and when the restaurant sent the busboy over to clean it, he removed a wad of money from his pocket and tipped the busboy. That confirmed he was indeed a baller. The baller made eye contact with her again. His eyes told her that he wanted her and that he was unhappy with Tacky Weave. He shifted his eyes onto his plate momentarily before looking back at Jada. Tacky Weave noticed that he was looking at something and she turned around to see Jada behind her.

"You see something you like?" she asked him.

Jada laughed at him from a far. The two finished their breakfast. Mr. Handsome flashed that big wad of money again before disappearing out of the restaurant. Jada just sat there picking at her breakfast. She wasn't really hungry, but she didn't want to go back to her room either. She needed to get the fuck out of this hotel. She hated living in hotels. She powered on her phone and checked her Instagram. She liked a picture of Starr and T.J. at the movies to see Avengers. This made her smile. She was so happy for Starr—happy that T.J. made her happy.

Even though she was having drama with Q, Jada was happy that Starr had someone to love in T.J. and happy that he loved her and called her mom. He even called Jada auntie. He was indeed a beautiful kid. She looked at the last picture she had posted. A picture of her in workout clothes and the Instagram trolls were out in full force.

Meechagirl 1212 said: *Jada is a Boss.*

Hotboy704 said: *Everything on her is fake.*

TMoney said: *Fake or Not shorty can get the D.*

Mr.ATL said: *Shorty always setting them thirst traps.*

Jada snapped a pic of her wine glass and her Louis bag. She captioned it: *Morning Mimosa. Then she paid her tab and made her way out into the lobby.*

In the lobby, she heard someone say, "Excuse me, Ms. Lady."

Couldn't these guys come up with an original line? She turned and came face to face with Mr. Handsome. Standing there with True Religion jeans, a Presidential Rolex and a Burberry shirt. He was indeed a boss. A guy like that could certainly understand a girl like her.

"What's up?"

"I saw you checking me out in the restaurant."

"Oh, I was checking you out? Whatever."

He laughed and said, "Don't be uptight. I was checking you out."

"You have a woman. And by the way, don't you think you should be worried about her walking up on you?"

"She's gone shopping with her sister."

"Oh, ok."

"What's your name?"

"Jada."

"I'm Tank."

"Good to meet you." She shook his hand and tried to walk around him but Tank jumped in front of her.

"What's your problem? I'm trying to go to my room."

She caught him staring at her ring finger.

"So, you're not married?"

"Do you see a ring?"

"Damn, you feisty. But I like it."

She liked his fine ass too but she was not about to let him know that.

"Can I talk to you for a second?"

"About what?"

"Look, let's just keep it real. I was looking at you but you were looking at me too."

"Okay, we made eye contact. You know that."

"We made more than I eye contact."

"What the hell are you talking about?"

"Our souls connected."

"Whatever. Tank, what do you want from me? You have a woman and I'm not about to play no side bitch role unless it's beneficial."

He laughed and said, "You're the kind of woman that likes to be taken care of?"

"I have before, but I'm not after money. I'm not about to be dealing with a nigga with a wife if I don't reap the benefits."

"I'm not married."

"Baby mama?"

"Yeah, she's one of them."

"Okay, you are one of them."

"One of who?"

"Hood legend."

"What the hell is a hood legend?"

"How many baby mamas you got?"

"Two."

"Okay, you don't qualify as a hood legend. Me and my friends say you're a hood legend if you have three."

He was laughing his ass off.

She smiled. She was still thinking about Fresh, wishing things could work out with him but Fresh had told her what he wanted and she had to respect it. "So, Tank, what did you want to talk about?"

"First of all, where are you from?"

"Atlanta. Born and raised. Where are you from?"

"Dade County."

"Miami?"

"You get down there much?"

"I used to go to South Beach from time to time. It's getting kind of played though."

"Yeah, I don't ever go there. People from Miami hate South Beach."

"I know you don't want to talk about South Beach."

"Damn, Jada, why are you so tough?"

"You don't know what tough is until you see the woman that raised me."

"I don't know the woman that raised you..." he glanced at her ass, "...but I wanna thank her. Goddamn I wanna thank her."

Jada laughed at him. Not only was he fine, but he was funny. She loved a man with a sense of humor.

"Where is the boyfriend?"

"I don't have one."

"Damn! Why not?"

"Well the last man I was with is doing time. I was seeing somebody, but he don't want to be in a relationship."

"What? I can't believe that."

"You know how y'all men do. Always wanting to play games."

"I don't play games."

"Nigga, you playing games now. Got that poor woman thinking that she in a relationship."

"Hey, a man will be a man."

"A man is going to play games."

"Can we keep in touch?"

"Depends."

"On what?"

"How am I going to benefit? I mean you are all the way in Miami."

"I just bought a home here. Just waiting on my furniture to be delivered."

"So you're going to be living in Atlanta?"

"Part time."

"Good."

"So, what's your number?"

"Is this going to be beneficial to me?"

"I think it will."

She gave him her number. He called her and she locked his number into her phone.

Chapter 21

NANA WAS CALLING BLACK BACK TO BACK AND HE SENT HER TO voicemail, but then his dad called. He ended the call with Sasha to talk to his dad.

"Hello?" Black said.

"Bring me my goddamned truck and bring my shit now!"

"What?"

"Nana just called me and told me that the police looking for yo ass. I want my goddamned truck now! I don't want to be involved with dem' white folks! Bring my shit now!"

"Okay, man, calm the fuck down."

"No, nigga. You calm the fuck down. I knew I shouldn't have gave you my shit in the first place. Bring me my shit now."

"I'm coming."

Black called Nana and she said, "Hey, the police has been here looking for you. They had a search warrant and they tore my house up. What the hell have you done?"

"Huh? Nothing, Nana," Black said as he wondered what they could have possibly wanted with him. It could have been a number of things. After all Shakur, Mike, Kenny-Boo and Tater were all dead and Popcorn, J.J. and Memphis had been murdered. He knew whatever it was that they were looking for him for, it could not be good.

"They didn't tell you what they wanted?"

"They wanted yo' black ass," Nana said, then she said, "Forgive me, Jesus, for cursing but I'm upset."

"Okay," Black said.

"Okay, what? You need to turn yourself in, Tyrann. Whatever you did, you can be forgiven for. But you need to turn yourself in and ask the Lord for forgiveness."

"Huh?"

"Huh, my ass," Nana said. "Forgive me, Lord."

"Nana, I gotta go now."

"Before you go. Have you spoken with yo daddy?"

"I have."

"Okay, remember what I said."

"Okay, Nana."

Black ended the call with Nana and drove to Bankhead Bo's house. Bo was waiting outside on the front porch smoking a cheap cigar, wearing overalls as usual. His hands were oily. He had just finished removing a transmission that he would sell for eight hundred dollars. Black got out of the car and approached the porch. Bo dropped his cigar and slapped the fuck out of Black. Black stumbled and Bo charged Black, grabbing Black's shirt and pulling it over his head.

Bo knew Black was too young and strong for his old ass, but he was Black's father and he could still outsmart the young punk motherfucker. Black, with the shirt over his head, couldn't see a damn thing and Bo kneed him in the balls. Black plummeted to the ground and Bo stomped on Black's head.

"What the fuck is your problem, man?" Black cried out.

As Black struggled to get on his feet, Bo put him in a headlock and started choking the fuck out him.

"I can't breathe."

"I don't give a fuck!"

Black gagged and Bo wanted to choke him out, but Black was his son and he knew how much Nana loved him so he released him then kicked him. "Punk motherfucka!"

Black stood on his feet and removed the shirt from covering his head. Black wanted to beat the fuck out of the old man. He knew he could but instead he dusted himself off and he said to Bo, "What the hell did you do that for?"

Bo held his guards by his face. "You wanna fight?"

"No, I don't wanna fight you. You're my pops. But don't put your hands on me no more."

"If I do, what are you gonna do? Beat my ass?"

"Yo, what the fuck is this all about? Why do you want to fight me?"

Bo lowered his guards and said, "I told you when I loaned you my truck, don't get in no bullshit. I should have known. You been getting in shit all of your life."

"What the hell are you talking about? You don't even know what the police want from me."

"You right, but I know it can't be good cuz, nigga, you ain't good."

"And like you were a good dad. You are the motherfucka I learned everything I know from."

Bo hopped on the porch and sat back in his seat and said, "Have a seat, son."

Black sat on the edge of the porch but kept his eye on his father. He was not going to take his eye off him again. He was not going to allow Bo to catch him off guard.

Bo said, "Look, man, I know I taught you everything I know and everything I did. What I did was wrong. I'm saying the way I went about shit was wrong. I am still a work in process."

"Process? You mean a work in progress?"

"You know what the fuck I meant."

"Okay."

"But the way I went about shit was wrong. I ran around here for years. Fucking all the women I laid eyes on and selling dope like it was legal until I got sent away. And I see you fuckin up, son, and you're fucking up bad. I was lucky. I was able to get out of the shit before it was too late. I was lucky I didn't have to spend the rest of my life in prison. Wait right here." Bo disappeared into the house and came back out with a shoebox and passed it to Black.

Black opened the shoebox and it was full to the top with money-order receipts.

"What is this all about? Why do you want me to see this?"

"These are receipts I sent my partners every month. I got six partners in the pen. They are my age and they are going to die in there. They ain't getting out. Do you want to die in the pen, son?"

"No."

"I don't know what the fuck you did. I don't know if it's too late or not, but if you get out of this shit, you need to sit yo ass down. Understand me?"

"I understand."

"And why don't you have a car?"

"Well, you know my car got shot up. The car was totaled. But it's in Rasheeda's name and I'm sure the insurance company has given her the check. But I don't even know how to ask her to get me another car."

"Yo sister is not going to do that. She said she will always love you but you keep getting her in all kinds of shit. She said she can't do you no more favors. Said something about she has restaurants in her name for you."

'She do."

"Why can't you just focus on the restaurants?"

"I don't know."

"I know. You're addicted to the lifestyle. You get a 'drenlin rush."

Black new his dad meant adrenaline but he wasn't about to correct him.

"You might be right."

"I am right."

"So you're going to give me a ride back to Atlanta?"

"Where are you going?"

"I don't know."

Sasha opened the door for Black and when she turned to walk away, Black slapped her on the ass.

"Boy, don't start nothing that you can't finish," she said with a smile.

He laughed as he stared at those P.I.N.K. Victoria secret shorts hugging her ass cheeks so nicely then he said, "Seriously, I need you to rent me a car."

"Why?" Sasha asked.

Black just stared at her. What the fuck was she doing asking him questions? Her job was to do whatever the fuck he asked. Not to question him. That's what she had always done before but now she was asking motherfuckin' questions.

She turned and faced him and those long nipples of hers were pointing directly at him. She was waiting on him to answer but he had lost his train of thought for a second as he stared at her chest.

"Why?" she said again.

"I need a car. That's why."

"How did you get here?"

"Look, why all the fucking questions?"

She walked away. She walked over to the window and looked outside then she turned to him and said, "You never tell me anything. Nothing. You know you came over a few weeks ago and you were on crutches?"

"Bout a month ago."

"What the fuck ever."

"What is your point?"

"You didn't tell me what happened. Did you notice I didn't ask? And that's the way it's always been. I don't ask questions. I just let you do whatever the fuck you want. Whenever you want."

"What do you mean, you let me do whatever I want? I am a grown-ass man. I do whatever I want."

"I know and that's the way it's always been with me and you."

"Look, are you going to get me a rental or not? I don't want to hear about all this bullshit. I just want to know if you're going to help me."

She sat down on the sofa and avoided eye contact with him.

He sat down beside her and said, "What's wrong?"

"He found out about you. I'm sorry, but that's why I'm acting like this."

"Your dad?"

"Yeah."

"What did he find out?"

"He found out that you were coming here. Those men that kidnapped you, he ordered it."

"How?"

"He apparently had the place bugged. He came in one day and told me about text messages that you and I had. Told me that you was a drug dealer and it was just a matter of time before the Feds get you."

"What? What about the shit that he has done? He ain't fucking goody-two shoes."

"You know how people are. Everybody likes to think their own shit don't stink."

"So you're not going to get me a rental?"

"Of course, I'm going to do it, baby."

"Well, why the questions?"

"I don't know why. I had a moment."

"But I do wonder. Why didn't you tell me that you had your car shot up?"

"How did you find out?"

"It was on the news. And the news said there was a female passenger. Who was she?"

Black looked her straight in the eyes and said, "My sister."

Chapter 22

HER NAME WAS CHANEL ANDREWS AND SHE SPELLED IT EXACTLY LIKE the luxury designer. Chanel was a five-foot, eight-inch amazon from Nashville, Tennessee and was twenty-nine years old. Her body was amazing. It was curvaceous with a super tiny waist. Her ass was big but not too big. Her flat stomach gave it the illusion of being bigger than it actually was. She had just a mouthful of breasts that sat up perfectly.

Chanel was employed at Delta Airlines and she did very well for herself, but she was accustomed to nice things. Her father and mother had made sure of that. She had attended private schools all through grade school and graduated from Duke University in North Carolina before moving to Atlanta. She rarely dated because most of the men thought she was stuck up, but in her mind, she wasn't stuck up. She was just accustomed to nice things and she wasn't going to settle for less. She was a real southern belle.

She was told to go to school and get an education to fall back on if she didn't marry rich, and so far, she couldn't find a man that satisfied her needs because of her huge demands. Chanel was taught that men took care of women. They opened doors. They pulled chairs out. They paid for tabs and walked on the outside.

She didn't mind her men being a little rough around the edges, but if they didn't take care of her and make her feel secure, they would never receive a second date.

Fresh's friend Brianna brought Chanel around and Fresh told her that he had the perfect man for her.

Fresh called Q and said, "I got somebody I want you to meet."

"I don't want to meet anyone."

"You gotta meet her, bruh. This woman has her own shit. She's not a gold digger."

"Look, I don't have time for bitches."

Fresh ended the call.

"So, is he coming over?" Chanel asked.

"Yes, but he wants a picture," Fresh lied.

Chanel posed. Her white dress that clung to her body. Her Chanel bag draped over her shoulder. Her naturally long hair flowed down to her shoulder. Fresh sent Q the pictures.

Seconds later, Q called back and Fresh stepped in the other room.

"Who the fuck is that?" Q asked.

"I am trying to tell you, bruh. This bitch is bad, homie."

"They're at your place right now?"

"Yes."

"I'll be there in an hour." After all Starr said that they were taking a break.

When Q met Chanel, she looked even more incredible than the picture. She shook his hand and soon afterward she rubbed sanitizer in the palm of her hand and she offered him some.

He accepted but looked at her like she was out to space. Was she trying to say that he was dirty? Who the fuck did she think she was? The Queen of England?

"I just have a thing for clean hands. I do this with my parents, too."

"So where are you from?

"Tennessee."

"Okay."

"Okay, what?" She smiled then crossed her leg. Q figured she was around twenty-eight, but she seemed to be mature.

"No man?"

"Nobody serious."

"But you date someone?"

"Don't everyone have somebody?"

She was right and he knew there was no way that this fine motherfucker wasn't fucking someone. Somebody was getting that kitty that's for damn sure.

"He's not doing what he's supposed to do?" Q asked.

"Let's not talk about him unless you want to talk about your girl."

"So what are you looking for? Just somebody to hang out with or something serious?"

"Look, I don't have time to play. So anybody that I go out with has to at least be a candidate for something serious. If not, then why waste my time?"

"I understand that, Ms. Chanel. You look a little high maintenance."

She laughed. "Why do you say that? Because I have nice things? Well, I can tell you this. Everything that I have on, I paid for with my own money.

Do I expect a man to treat me nice? Yes, that's the way I was raised but I can take care of myself and what I can't do for myself, my daddy can do."

"Daddy's girl?"

"Better believe it."

"Fresh wants to go to the Hawks game. Y'all coming with us tomorrow."

"Is that an invite?"

"Yes."

"Well, we're coming but I don't sit in Heaven."

"Huh?"

"I like to sit in the first four rows. Otherwise, what's the point?"

He laughed and said, "We sit on the floor, baby."

"I can do that."

Chapter 23

JADA WAS IN HER ROOM WHEN THE PHONE RANG. IT WAS TANK.
Damn! He was calling already. She was glad he called, but she didn't want to answer on the first ring. She didn't want him to think that she was thirsty.

"Hey!" Jada said.

"What you doing?"

"Just resting. You?"

"Calling to see if you wanted to meet for dinner. Can you get away?"

She laughed and said, "Can I get away? You're the one with the chick. Can you get away?"

"She's with her sister."

"Where do you want to meet?"

"Doesn't matter to me. You like to eat?"

"Who don't like to eat?"

"I was actually thinking about going to the gun range. You wanna go and shoot?"

"That's different."

"You don't have no record do you?"

"No, the question is do you have a record?"

"Look, my friend works at the range, so don't worry about me."

"What? If I had a record, then I would be fucked? Your friend works there but you said 'don't worry about you.'"

He laughed and said, "I guess I worded that shit pretty fucked up."

"You worded it very fucked up." Then she paused and said. "I don't think they check your record to rent a gun for the range."

"They don't but sometimes police ask for a list of people that used the range at random. One of my friends is in prison right now because of it."

"Damn I didn't know that."

He laughed and said, "I'll come pick you up."

"Okay, I'm just going to throw on some jeans and some sneakers."

"I'm sure you will look sexy in whatever you decide to wear."

Jada was wearing jeans and a pair of pink Jordan's with a baseball hat. Tank arrived in a black Porsche 911 wearing gold-plated old-school Gazal's. Jada jumped on the other side of the car and was about to take a selfie when Tank said, "Whoa!"

Jada laughed and said, "Chill the fuck out. You ain't in the selfie. All you can see is your black T-shirt."

He said, "Let me see."

The pic just showed a smiling-ass Jada and Tank's T-shirt and his arm. There were no tats on his right arm, so there was no way anybody could know it was him.

"I knew you was about to post this shit on Instagram."

"You better believe it."

"How many followers do you have?"

"Last time I checked, I think it was close to a hundred thousand."

"Damn."

"How many you got?"

"I ain't on social media. Waste too much time. Can't get the real work done."

"What is the real work?"

He laughed. "Wait until we get to know each other first."

"I got an idea."

"What do you think I do?"

"Either a music producer, in real estate or a concert promoter."

He was laughing his ass off. "Wrong. Wrong and Wrong."

Jada laughed and said, "Can I post my pic, please, sir?"

"Post it."

Jada posted her picture then she turned her attention back to Tank and said, "You're not going to try to kill me, are you?"

He looked at her thighs and then licked his lips and said, "I wanna kill you all right."

She slapped him playfully and said, "That's not what I'm talking about, silly."

"I ain't no killer. But don't push me."

"Revenge is the sweetest thing next to getting pussy," Jada said.

"Huh?"

"Tupac. You don't know your old school, young boy?"

"I'm older than you. How old are you anyway?"

"Around thirty but I'm an old soul."

"I'm thirty-four."

"Okay, you're young. Just like I thought."

"What?" He laughed."

"Though you're thirty-four, I bet I'm more mature than yo' ass," Jada said.

"Maybe."

"You look like an old Madden-playing-ass nigga."

"You think you know me?"

Jada laughed and said, "Tell me you don't play video games."

"Okay I might play every now and then."

And they both laughed their asses off.

"So you take all your girls to the gun range on the first date?"

"All what girls?"

"Nigga, don't give me that. The first time I saw you, you was with your baby mama."

"Honestly, I don't have time for a lot of women. Plus, my girl can fight."

"Guess what? That makes two of us. So if she comes running in my face. I'm going to see if she can really fight."

"It's not going to get down to that."

"I hope not because I don't start shit but I will damn sure finish it."

When they arrived at the gun range, the instructor gave them shooting instructions and provided them both with targets. They both fired thirty times and Jada was the more accurate. She hit her target fifteen out of thirty shots.

Tank turned to her and said, "Damn, you're accurate as hell."

"Yeah, so now you know not to fuck with me."

"I don't hit women."

"That woman of yours who you said can fight so well?" She paused. "Now you know to tell her to stay the fuck away from me."

He laughed and said, "Or else you'll kill her?"

"Look, the difference between me and her is that I'm crazy. So even if I get my ass beat, I'll still keep coming. But I don't know what getting my ass beat feels like."

"You're a boss, huh?"

"An absolute boss."

"I feel you."

After they finished shooting, they sat in his car and talked. He placed his hand on her thigh and she slapped the fuck out of him.

He held his jaw and said, "What was that all about?"

"I should be asking you."

"I was just rubbing your leg for you."

"I don't need my leg rubbed."

There was an awkward silence before he said, "So how did you like the date?"

"It was something different and you seem cool. We'll see how it goes."

"What do you mean 'we'll see how it goes'?"

She lowered the music and said, "Well, if you think taking me to a shooting range is going to make me be somebody's side bitch, you got another thing coming."

"I hate that word."

"What word?"

"Side bitch."

"I call it like I see it."

"I see."

"But playing number two comes at a cost. I'm not cheap, baby."

"You all about the money?"

"What? I have my own money. I'm moving into a luxury townhome. I drive foreign cars and I don't need nobody for shit."

Which was true, Jada still had lots of the money that Shamari had left her and Big Papa had been paying her bills before he was murdered.

"If it's not about the money, what is it about?"

"I never said it wasn't about the money, but it's not all about the money. Look, why are we arguing about this? All I'm saying is that I'm not going to be number two if you can't help a bitch out."

"What do you need help with?"

"Well, for starters. I'm moving to a new place this weekend and I'm going to need a handyman to help me put my shit together and movers. Can you help with that?"

"Not a problem. Now do you need your thigh rubbed?"

"Boy, bye." Jada laughed.

●   ●   ●

The next day the Hawks were playing the Heat. Fresh, Brianna, Q and Chanel sat on the floor on the Hawks side of the gym.

Fresh whispered in Q's ear. "Last time I was at a basketball game, the Rockets were playing the Mavs and I was creeping on my baby mama with this chick named Shawna. They put my ass on the Jumbotron and one of my baby mama's friends spotted me and told her. Be careful of the Jumbotron."

"I ain't hiding from nobody. Starr said we were taking a break. So we're taking a break."

"I feel ya."

At halftime, Q and Fresh went to the concession stand to pick up some hot dogs and that's when Fresh spotted Jada with some dude standing in the concession line. He couldn't believe this bitch had moved on with her life so fast. He wanted to speak to her but he didn't want to make a big scene because he didn't want her to go and tell Starr that Q was there with a woman. Though they weren't together right now, he didn't want the drama for his friend. But he sent Jada a text just to see if she would lie.

Fresh: *Where you at?*
Jada: *Can I get a hey first?*
Fresh: *My bad. How are you?*
Jada: *I'm good. I'm at the Hawks game with a friend.*
Fresh: *With a guy?*
Jada: *Ummmm Yeah...Why?*
Fresh: *Just asking.*
Jada: *Talk to you later. The second half is about to start.*

Fresh couldn't eat his food. He kept looking at Jada and the guy laughing and having a good time and that shit had him fuming. But he was the one that had told her that he didn't want to be in a relationship and so he had to accept it.

Chapter 24

WHEN BLACK ANSWERED THE PHONE TETE SAID, "GET YOUR KIDS AND let's take them to the movies. Butterfly keeps saying that she wants to meet your daughter and that you promised that you were going to take them to the movies to see the Avengers." TeTe was lying across her bed facetiming Black.

"Bae, I want to, but—"

"But what? Black, you only have one life and you better spend it with the people that love you and that you love."

"You're right, babe. Let me call their baby mama and tell them that I want to take them to the movies. She can be difficult sometimes, you know?"

"Call her and call me back and let me know what she says."

TeTe terminated the call and stripped down naked. She was about to hop into the shower when she got a call from Black. The baby mama said it was okay and that he would come to pick her and Butterfly up at six. They would ride over to pick the kids up together.

TeTe never expected Black to bring her around his baby mama. Some dudes were funny about shit like that. She would make sure that she was fly as hell. She expected the baby mama to be younger than she was, but she would make sure the bitch knew that she was no competition.

Black picked her up and as soon as he laid eyes on her, he said, "You look delicious, baby." TeTe was wearing a pair of white skinny jeans and a Blue Blazer and black YSL heels. Simple but elegant.

She smiled and said, "We'll see about that at the end of the night."

Butterfly laughed and TeTe was sure her grown ass knew that she and Black were talking about having sex. Kids today were much more advanced and Butterfly was absolutely too grown for her own good. When they were on the way to Asia's house to pick up the kids, Chris Brown was playing on Pandora.

Butterfly said, "So, what is your daughter's name again?"

"Tierany."

Butterfly smiled. "I can't wait to meet her."

"I told her about you too," Black lied.

"He has a son too. Man-Man." TeTe laughed and said, "Why in the world did y'all call that boy Man-Man?"

"The same reason they call you TeTe."

Butterfly laughed.

TeTe said, "You got me on that one. I hated TeTe when I was growing up but then when I saw that the name wasn't going anywhere, I got used to it. I don't think about it at all now. Well, I don't want to call your son Man-Man. What the hell is his real name?"

"His name is Tyrann. Just like my name."

"I'm going to call him Tyrann."

"But you're going to keep calling me Black?"

"I like Black. I love your big black—"

Butterfly laughed and TeTe shot her a look to let her know that she was being too fast, but did the girl really have a choice. The child had seen everything. She knew her mother was a madam though she didn't know the term for it. She knew that her mother collected money from prostitutes. She had overheard her more than once demanding money from the girls, even cursing them out.

And one of her older cousins Christian had told her that her mom was a pimp. Butterfly had asked her mother what a pimp was and TeTe demanded that she tell her where she heard that word. After Butterfly told where she learned the word, TeTe cursed the boy out.

Black arrived at Asia's house and pulled into the driveway. TeTe was about to get out of the car. She wanted to see Black's taste in women. She wanted to see her competition.

But Black said, "Chill! Stay in the car. I don't want no drama."

"Well, you shouldn't have picked us up. Why can't I come in?"

Black said, "Look, baby. Trust me. It will be easier. I mean once she sees how good you look and the fact that you're an upgrade on her, I'm going to have problems."

"Just hurry up."

"Look, it's only going to be a few minutes. The kids are ready."

"Well, you should have just called the bitch and let them run out of the house. It would be a lot easier."

"I have to take a piss."

"Take yo piss then and while you at it, get some head. I don't give a fuck what you do."

Butterfly laughed. She thought her Mama was funny.

Black entered Asia's house and Asia was brushing Tierany's hair and Man-Man was applying lotion on his legs. Both kids wore shorts and Avengers T-shirts.

Black said, "Can you hurry up? I have someone waiting on us."

Asia said, "Your bitch?"

"Look, I don't have time to argue with you."

"We ain't arguing." Asia finished brushing Tierany's hair and wrapped it with a purple scrunchie.

Black said, "Come on. Let's go."

Black was making a beeline to the door with the children following him when Asia trailing them yelled, "I hope you don't think I'm going to let my kids go somewhere with someone I ain't never met before!"

Black turned to her and said, "Look. I'll introduce you when I get back. We're going to be late for the movies."

"Whatever!"

When Black and the children were about to get into the car, Asia approached the passenger side of the car and TeTe gave Asia a once over and decided real fast that this bitch wasn't on her level. She was wearing a cheap-ass Wal-Mart t-shirt and a pair of gym shorts. Her hair was nice but unkempt. One of those black girls that tried her best to look like she was mixed, but she looked real basic to TeTe. TeTe lowered the window and gave Asia a fake smile.

Asia said, "I'm Asia who are you?"

"The Black Widow." TeTe laughed.

"Does the Black Widow have a name?" Asia looked as if she was pissed.

"Lighten up Asia, It was just a joke, I'm TeTe. Good to meet you."

"Those are my kids."

"They will be in good hands."

Asia looked at Black who was looking annoyed as hell. Wanting to hurry the hell up before these two crazy bitches decide they didn't like each other.

Asia said, "That's all I wanted. I just wanted to meet TeTe."

"Well, I told him that I wanted to come in and meet you."

Asia said, "Why didn't you invite her in?"

"Look, we're pressed for time." Man-Man and Tierany climbed in the backseat of the rental.

"Good to meet you, Asia."

Asia said, "Let me give you my number, TeTe. Just in case you need to call me."

"Oh hell no! She don't need your number." He paused and said, "For what?"

Asia ignored Black's ass and was about to give TeTe the number. TeTe had the phone in her hand waiting on the phone number when Black ran to the passenger side and wedged himself between the women. Seconds later, an unmarked car drove up and right after that two Atlanta police cars came right behind them.

Two detectives approached Black and Black recognized them. They were the same two clowns that had approached him at Nana's house months ago before Lani was murdered—Williams and Kearns.

Williams flashed his badge and said, "Tyrann, can I speak to you for a second?"

"For what?"

Seconds later, TeTe hopped out of the car and said, "What the fuck do you want with him?"

Kearns said, "He's under arrest."

Four other uniformed cops were now out of their cars; an Asian, a white and two more black officers. Black recognized one of the uniformed cops. The white one was Chad Bailey. He and Black had played on the same football team in middle school and he had seen him over the years. Bailey was a tall gangly looking white guy with a goatee. He'd always hung around Black guys in the hood and played sports with them growing up and he even spoke with a black dialect.

Black said, "Bailey, what the fuck is going on?"

"I was just called for backup. I have no idea what's going on."

TeTe said, "He's under arrest for what? He hasn't done anything. We're on our way to the goddamn movies and you come with this bullshit? You wanna lock somebody up in front of their kids? Who the fuck does that?"

"He's got more to worry about than what his kids think of him," Williams said.

TeTe said, "Ok, but what the fuck do you want with him?" Then she turned to Asia and said, "You have something to do with this?"

"I don't know what you're talking about. I wanna know what this is all about myself."

"Triple homicide."

"What? I ain't killed nobody."

Williams removed his cuffs and ordered Black to turn around. Then he handcuffed him. Black was lying face down on the hood of the car as they searched him for weapons. They removed his keys, a wad of cash and two condoms.

Tierany sprang from the car and ran to her daddy, grabbing his legs.

"Baby, step back," Black said.

Tierany wouldn't let go of his leg. "Don't take my daddy to jail."

Man-Man got out of the car and ran up to Asia. "Mommy, why are they taking daddy to jail?"

Asia ordered her kids inside the house. Butterfly was in the backseat crying.

TeTe said, "Don't worry. I'm going to get you out as soon as you get downtown. I don't give a fuck how much it cost."

One of the officers said, "Whatever. Nobody gets out for triple murder."

Chad Bailey and another officer escorted Black to Bailey's squad car. The two plain-clothes officers jumped in their car and drove away.

When Bailey was about to drive away, Black said, "Bailey, can you do me a favor?"

"What?"

"Can you loosen the cuffs? They're cutting my circulation off."

Bailey opened the back door and loosened the cuffs. Black felt much better and then he said, "Can I talk to my lady for one minute, Bailey? I swear to God there will be no funny stuff."

Bailey made eye contact with Black. There was fifteen years of friendship between them, and even though he knew Black was a known drug dealer, every time that he'd seen Black, Black gave him nothing but respect. His partner, a rookie cop named Stevens, looked on.

He said, "I'm going to leave you cuffed and have my gun drawn. If you run, Tyrann, I swear to God, I'm going to have to bust a cap in your ass." He turned to Stevens and said, "It's going to be okay."

"I'm not going to run, Bailey. I swear."

Bailey helped Black out of the car. Black called TeTe over and they stood at the rear of the car.

Bailey stood ten feet away with his weapon drawn. Black said, "You have my keys."

"Yes."

"There is a house key on the chain. My address is 9565 Eden Ridge Lane. I have a man in my basement that I have been torturing for the last month."

"What?"

"I know it sounds crazy."

"Hell the fuck yeah."

Bailey said, "Hurry up."

"Look, I need you to get rid of him. Any kind of way that you can. He can't be in my house. I don't know when or if I'm going to get out of this shit. So help me out. Please, help me out."

"I'll take care of it."

Black turned to Bailey and said, "Thank you."

Bailey grabbed Black by the arm and helped him into the back of the patrol car and they drove away.

TeTe phoned Butterfly's nanny, Auntie Lucille, whom she had given the day off and ordered her to get her ass to her house right away. TeTe told her it was an emergency and it was. She was needed to watch Butterfly while TeTe went to Black's house to get that man out of his basement. Black was charged with triple murder and she knew that he needed her now more than anything to come through for him.

Auntie Lucille was running fifteen minutes behind and TeTe was furious that she had been so late. When she finally arrived, TeTe cursed her out and jumped in the Tesla when the phone rang. It was a number that she didn't recognize.

"Hello?"

"It's Rachel."

"Who the fuck is Rachel? I don't know no goddamned Rachel."

"Cassandra's friend."

"I don't know no motherfuckin' Cassandra."

"Remember we met at Panera a few days ago?"

TeTe said, "Oh, I'm sorry, baby. I got a lot on my mind." It dawned on TeTe that Rachel was out with a client.

"Is everything okay?"

"No, it's not okay."

"What do you mean?"

"Well the client hasn't paid me all the money. Telling me that he has to go to the bank in the morning. Saying that he doesn't have the cash on him. I know you had said that he would pay half on the credit card and the other half in cash."

"Yes," TeTe huffed. "That's exactly what I said. Look, I don't have time for this shit today but don't let him leave. Take his keys if you have to." TeTe wasn't worried. She knew she would get the money. He always tried this bullshit.

"Scream rape if you have to. I have something I have to do, so keep him there any kind of way you can. As a matter of fact, I'm going to send Jada down there to help you."

"Who?"

"Jada, the girl that was with me."

"Oh, that bitch."

"Look, I ain't got no time for an attitude. I need you to not let his ass leave that room. I'm going to need at least two hours."

"Okay."

"What room are you in?"

"1532."

TeTe was impressed with the outside of Black's home, but on the inside it was cold as if nobody lived there. It certainly wasn't warm and inviting like her home. It had basic furniture and a lot of TVs like most men's home, but there were no pictures. No art. Nothing to make you want to be there. But again, Black was a man and this is how men lived. She bet there was no food or very little food in his place.

TeTe and Country were there to do Black a favor and she still couldn't believe that he'd asked her to get rid of a man that was in his basement. The good thing about Black's home was that the lot was huge, so it would be easy to remove the man from the home without some nosey-ass-wanna-be-hero neighbor getting all up in their business.

TeTe and Country had been inside for twenty minutes before they found the stairs that led to the basement. They walked slowly downstairs and when they reached the bottom, they spotted a huge cage, bed covers, panties, baby oil, old spoiled ramen noodles and buckets of urine. But there was no sign of a person. The cage was wide open. Where in the hell was the captive, she thought as she examined the scene. Wondering what the fuck had gone on in here. Was Black into some sick demented sex slave fetishes? But more than that, where in the hell was this person that she was supposed to get?

Jada had been asleep when TeTe called her and told her to get down to1532 to help Miss America. She'd said something about a client refusing to pay and the plan was to tease the motherfucker like she was going to give him some head. TeTe wanted Jada to stall him until she got there. She didn't want to do it but TeTe had been good to her and she was paying for the room until she moved so she agreed to help out. But, she thought to herself, what kind of man would even be interested in Miss America? She knocked on the door. But nobody was responding. She heard voices. They were having a conversation. She was begging him not to go and he said he had to go and that he would be right back with the money. In the background, Jada could hear Steve Harvey. Family Feud was on.

She tapped on the door again and then she heard a male voice say, "Did you order room service?"

"No."

"Well someone is at the door."

Jada could hear the sound of high heels coming toward the door. Seconds later, Miss. America stood before her, even more beautiful than before. She was wearing a blond wig and not a whole lot of makeup. A white form fitting dress wrapped her body and her tits were about to explode. She stepped outside and said, "Look I'm sorry. I know you don't want to be here."

Jada didn't like the bitch or her gorilla-looking friend trying to pretend to be a woman but she had to put her feelings aside. She was there for TeTe.

Jada said, "What's going on?"

"Well, the short version of the story is that he don't want to pay and TeTe told me to make sure he doesn't leave. So if you could help me seduce him until TeTe gets here, I would appreciate it."

Jada sighed and said, "Let's go inside."

When Miss America stepped inside the room, the client had his back turned and he was watching TV. A commercial break from Family Feud came on.

Miss America said, "I have a guest."

The man turned and faced Jada and her mouth flew wide open.

"Yeah, I would like for you to meet—."

"This motherfucker knows exactly who I am! Dr. Craig Matthews. You've graduated from fucking strippers and snorting coke to fuckin' trannys and coke. What the fuck?"

To be continued

GET A FREE eBOOK!

Enjoyed this book?
If you enjoyed this book please write a review and email it to me at
kevinelliott3@gmail.com, and get a FREE ebook.

K. Elliott Book Order Form
PO Box 12714
Charlotte NC 28220

Book Name	Quantity	Price	Shipping/ Handling	Total
Dear Summer		X $14.95	+ $3.00 per book	
Dilemma		X $14.95	+ $3.00 per book	
Entangled		X $13.95	+ $3.00 per book	
Godsend Series 1–5		X $14.95	+ $3.00 per book	
Godsend Series 6–10		X $14.95	+ $3.00 per book	
Kingpin Wifeys Vol. 1		X $14.95	+ $3.00 per book	
Kingpin Wifeys Vol. 2		X $14.95	+ $3.00 per book	
Kingpin Wifeys Vol. 3		X $14.95	+ $3.00 per book	
Kingpin Wifeys Vol. 4		X $14.95	+ $3.00 per book	
Kingpin Wifeys Vol. 5		X $14.95	+ $3.00 per book	
Kingpin Wifeys Vol. 6		X $14.95	+ $3.00 per book	
Street Fame		X $14.95	+ $3.00 per book	
Treasure Hunter		X $15.00	+ $3.00 per book	
			TOTAL	

Mailing Address

Name:

Mailing Address:

City	State	Zip

Method Of Payment
[   ] Check [   ] Money Order

Thank you for your support

About the Author

K. Elliott, aka The Well Fed Black Writer, penned his first novel, Entangled, in 2003. Although he was offered multiple signing deals, Elliott decided to found his own publishing company, Urban Lifestyle Press.

Bookstore by bookstore, street vendor by street vendor, Elliott took to the road selling his story. He did not go unnoticed, selling 50,000 units in his first year and earning a spot on the Essence Magazine Bestsellers list.

Since Entangled, Elliott has published five titles of his own and two more on behalf of authors signed to Urban Lifestyle Press. For one book, The Ski Mask Way, Elliott was selected to co-author with hip-hop superstar 50 Cent. Along the way, he has continued to look for innovative ways to push his books to his fans while keeping down his overhead.

Elliott is passionate about sharing what he has learned with aspiring authors, and has conducted learning webinars filled with information on what works best for him. He is the author of numerous best-sellers including Dilemma, Street Fame, Treasure Hunter, Dear Summer, Entangled, The Godsend Series and the hugely intriguing Kingpin Wifeys Series.

5/17

CPSIA information can be obtained
at www.ICGtesting.com
Printed in the USA
LVOW07s2050150517
534584LV00010B/1890/P

9 780997 455168